SKELETON IN SEARCH

OF A CLOSET

By E. X. Ferrars

SKELETON IN
SEARCH OF A CLOSET

E. X. FERRARS

PUBLISHED FOR THE CRIME CLUB BY
DOUBLEDAY & COMPANY, INC.
GARDEN CITY, NEW YORK
1982

Library of Congress Cataloging in Publication Data

Ferrars, E. X.
    Skeleton in search of a closet.

    I. Title.
PR6003.R458S5   1982   823'.912
ISBN 0-385-18268-6   AACR2
Library of Congress Catalog Card Number 82–45355

First Edition in the United States of America

SKELETON IN SEARCH
OF A CLOSET

CHAPTER 1

The typewriter upstairs had been silent for some time. That was a bad sign. When Peter got stuck, when the ideas would not come, when the page in the typewriter stayed blank, he was liable to emerge presently from his room in a kind of mood which always had a very depressing effect on me. I had been married to him for two years and still had not learnt the knack of ignoring these black moods, even though I knew they seldom lasted long, sometimes for no more than an hour or two.

I knew that anxiety was at the bottom of them, because the wolf was never very far from our door. Yet when, as occasionally happened, they continued for several days, sooner or later I would find myself with a sense that they must be somehow my fault and would not fade until I had discovered what I had done or not done to cause them. But although I was quite well aware that in reality they had nothing to do with me, this was almost as upsetting as believing that I was to blame, for while depression had him in its grip I felt that I hardly existed for him. I was very much in love with him, and I could go through agonies of anxiety when it began to seem as if nothing that I could do would ever penetrate his always courteous but implacable withdrawal.

To take my mind off the silence upstairs, I settled down by the fire in the living-room with several cookery books and started looking for promising recipes which I had not tried before. I was fond of cooking and to help out finan-cially when Peter had given up his job in journalism and

settled down to full-time writing, I had started a small catering service, working in a kitchen which we had made the
most up-to-date part of the old cottage which I had recently inherited from my father, and delivering in a fitted
van the dishes that had been ordered by families in the
neighbourhood for parties that they were giving. I had built
up a fair reputation and often had more work than I could
cope with. With Christmas coming in another three weeks I
had already been turning down orders.

But it happened that on this Saturday afternoon I had
nothing to do, so it seemed a good time for searching for
new ideas for when the party season really got going. I was
in the middle of reading a recipe for duck *à la Creole* when
the doorbell rang.

I stood up and crossed to the front door, which opened
straight from the small garden into the living-room, pushed
back the velvet curtain that covered it in the hope of keeping out draughts, and lifting the latch, let in a spray of
rain, a buffet of a bitterly cold wind and my sister-in-law,
Beryl.

Beryl Cosgrove was Peter's younger sister and she lived
with their stepmother in the old thatched house that we
could just see from our windows and in which I had first
met Peter. He had been at Oxford then and I had been ten
years old. For several years after that I had seen him from
time to time, but it had been a long while before, all of a
sudden, we had become aware of one another as a man
and a woman. When that had happened I had just given up
my job in a bookshop in nearby Alcaster to look after my
father, who had had a severe stroke and had had to retire
from his work as curator of Alcaster's small museum. He
had died only a year later and by then Peter and I had
been on the verge of marriage. The cottage where I had
lived for most of my life was mine, and together we had decided that Peter should give up his job and settle into the
cottage with me.

Slamming the door shut against the wind and rain, I drew the curtain over it again while Beryl went quickly to the fire, taking off the plastic hood that she was wearing and shaking raindrops from it onto the hearth. They made a little hissing noise as they splashed into the flames. She was thirty-eight, with curly reddish hair, like Peter's, though there the resemblance between them ended. She was small and tended to plumpness, whereas everything about him was long and narrow and bony. Beryl's hazel eyes were slightly prominent, and she wore round, rimless glasses. She worked in the museum of which my father had been curator and she lived apparently contentedly with Henrietta, her stepmother, who had been a widow for fifteen years and for whom Beryl's companionship was an obvious blessing, just as it was convenient for Beryl to have a home where she could live very cheaply and be well looked after.

"Let me take your coat," I said, and when Beryl took it off and handed it to me, I took it out to the kitchen and hung it on a peg. The kitchen and the living-room were the only rooms on the ground floor, and there was a staircase going up between them to the narrow passage and the three rooms and small bathroom overhead. Standing at the bottom of the stairs for a moment, I listened. The typewriter was still silent.

When I returned to the living-room, Beryl said, "I've only come for a minute, Freda. There's something I wanted to talk over with you. I suppose you know Wednesday week is Henrietta's eightieth birthday."

"Wednesday week?" We both sat down on either side of the fire. "I knew it was sometime soon," I said, "but I wasn't sure of the exact date. Are we doing anything about it?"

"That's what I wanted to discuss with you," Beryl said. "We're having a family lunch party. Everyone's coming, and I thought perhaps you'd do the catering for it. I've arranged to have the day off from the museum, but I'd never have the time to lay on a worthwhile meal. Anyway, I'm no good at that sort of thing and you're so clever. Will you do it?"

"You say everyone's coming," I said. "Does that mean Martin, Luke and Vanessa?"

"Yes, and of course Grace."

"It's a bit of a triumph to get Martin to come, isn't it? He always seems too grand for us."

Martin Cosgrove, the extremely successful actor who it was generally thought would soon achieve a knighthood, was the only one of Henrietta's collection of stepchildren whom I hardly knew. Henrietta had five stepchildren. Her husband, Raymond, who had been a professor of history at a northern university, had married three times and had had three children, Grace, Martin and Luke, by his first wife, and Peter and Beryl by his second. So when he had died he had left Henrietta with a considerable family, which by then included Luke's wife, Vanessa. Henrietta had been sixty when she married Raymond Cosgrove. She had been the widow of an old friend of his, but had had no children of her own. They had come to live in the old house in the village of Ickfield twenty years ago. I remember how intrigued I was at being told that this aged couple had only just got married and had just returned to England after a honeymoon that had lasted a year and taken them round the world. I had not known that it was possible to get married when you were so very old. But Henrietta had been a young sixty, as she was now a surprisingly young eighty, and I had soon adopted her, with great affection, as an honorary aunt.

I had never had much contact with the professor. He had always been a shadowy figure to me, usually half-hidden behind heaps of books and uncontrolled piles of papers, and when he had died five years later the fact had made scarcely any impression on me. Now I could hardly remember him. It seemed to me simply that it had only been Henrietta and Beryl who had been friends and neighbours for nearly all my life.

"I'll do what I can," I said. "D'you want it hot or cold?"

"I'll leave that entirely to you," Beryl answered. "The main thing is, we want it to be a surprise for Henrietta. That's partly why I'd like you to do the job. If I suddenly get awfully busy in the house, doing lots of cooking, she'll naturally know what's up. But if you can get everything ready here and bring it over in the morning about the time the others start arriving, it'll be the surprise I want it to be."

"Let's see, how many will there be? Henrietta and you and Martin and Luke and Vanessa and Grace—"

"And you and Peter. That's eight."

"Nobody else? No friends from the village?"

"No, as I said, I think it should just be family."

"Will they all be staying with you?"

"Good Lord no, none of them. I've the day off, but I've got a job to do. I simply couldn't cope. Martin and Luke and Vanessa will be staying with Grace."

Grace Kenworthy was Raymond Cosgrove's oldest and favourite child. It had been to be near her that he and Henrietta had come to live in Ickfield when he retired. Grace's husband, Edmund, had been a doctor in Alcaster, but their home had been in Ickfield, a rambling and slightly ramshackle but attractive Georgian house, facing the village green. Since his death in a car crash three years ago, when he had been called out late at night in a thick fog when the roads were icy, she had lived on there alone and had plenty of room for her brothers and her sister-in-law.

Luke, like Martin, had begun life as an actor, but he had recognized fairly quickly that he had not much talent and that his brother would always outshine him. When he married, he had joined Vanessa in the very successful interior decorating business that she was running, and had been ready, being a naturally idle person, to let her go on running it. They were fairly frequent visitors in Ickfield, which, they both said, gave them a wonderful escape from the pressures of their London lives. Of all the Cosgroves it was only Martin who had no interest in, or perhaps had never really accepted his second stepmother.

"Of course, we'd like a cake, if you can manage it," Beryl said.

"With eighty candles?"

She laughed. "Well no, I thought just one in the middle for Henrietta to blow out and make her wish."

"I wonder what that wish will be."

"I think I can tell you that. It's that I should get married before she dies. She worries about me, you know. She can't believe I'm perfectly happy with my job and that I'm quite satisfied with my pay. It doesn't seem natural to her. I try to get her to understand that I feel I'm unusually lucky to have work I enjoy so much. If course, the atmosphere of the place hasn't been the same since we lost your father. Max is all right, he does his best, I've a great regard for him, but he'll never have your father's personality."

I agreed with her, though I liked Max Ormerod. He was my father's successor as curator of the Alcaster Museum. He was a very shy man whose whole mind seemed to be absorbed in the excavation of a Roman villa in the neighbourhood. It was not a very notable villa. The Roman who had built it could not have been a very notable Roman. But occasionally an interesting find was made, some battered fragments of mosaic paving, a cache of coins, and when this happened Max would become vivid and excited and exhilarated. Beryl had next to no interest in the villa. She was the librarian in the museum, in charge of her department.

She stood up. "So it's arranged, isn't it? I'm so grateful to you for managing. And remember, not a word to

Henrietta. I think I can get the table laid without her knowing, or anyway, get the glasses and everything ready to put out. And I'll see to the drinks, that's easy. I do hope you think it's a nice idea. Grace doesn't, you know. She's against it. But she's agreed to have the others to stay with her and to help as much as she can. She always likes having them, and though she pretends she isn't, I think she's specially pleased that Martin's coming. I believe she suggested to him on the telephone that he should bring his latest woman, but I gather that didn't go down too well. A pity. I expect Henrietta would have enjoyed meeting her. She's still as interested in people as she ever was. It's wonderful, really, isn't it?"

"Why doesn't Grace like the idea of the party?" I asked.

"Well, I think she'd like it all right if she'd thought of it herself," Beryl said. "She does so love to run things. Well, goodbye, and thank you again."

I fetched her coat and she went out into the rain and the gathering darkness.

As she left, the typewriter upstairs started again. For a little while it clattered rapidly, then paused, then went on once more. Relieved, I went back to my cookery books. I began to think about the lunch party for Henrietta's birthday and what I might cook for it. If the weather continued as cold as it was at present, a hot meal would be welcome and with our van, with its heated chambers, I could easily provide one. But if the matter was really to be kept a secret from Henrietta until the last moment, a cold meal would be simpler to organize. I was pondering this when the typewriter stopped, footsteps sounded crossing the floor overhead and Peter came downstairs.

Although he was forty, ten years older than I was, he looked a good deal younger than that. There was a kind of immaturity about his long, narrow face, a sort of innocence in the gaze of his very bright blue eyes, which I believed he would never lose, even when wrinkles, which were just beginning to show, had grown deep from nostrils to mouth and crisscrossed his slightly hollow cheeks. His curly reddish hair stood straight up from his forehead in more of a thatch than I approved of, but it was very difficult to persuade him to have it cut. Day after day, when I badgered him enough about it, he would promise to go into Alcaster to have the job done, but sometimes weeks would pass before he finally gave in and went, to come back with it cropped almost to his skull. He was utterly indifferent to his appearance, which was a pity because he was really a very good-looking man. He was tall, very slender, and although he looked so bony, he moved with charmingly casual ease. He was dressed more or less as I was in old corduroy slacks and a sweater, but his had not been to the cleaner's for a far longer time than mine. To deprive him of his favourite clothes, even briefly, took art and determination.

Crossing the room, he dropped into the chair where Beryl had sat and stretched out his long legs. He was looking satisfied.

"I've thought of a title at last," he said. "I was getting worried, now that I'm so near the end of the damned thing, that one hadn't come to me. *The Screaming Spires*. What do you think of it?"

I considered it.

"A bit esoteric," I suggested.

"But I like the sound of it, and it happens to fit the story. I don't think it matters all that much if people don't know where it comes from."

I had not read any of the book. Peter never allowed me to do that until he had finished. All I knew about it was that, like his first two novels, *Quiet Dies the Don*, and *Home of Lost Corpses*, it was based on his memories of Oxford.

"But to tell the truth, Freda, I'm getting tired of these

Oxford yarns," he went on. "I think my next one will be in an African republic."

"You've never been to Africa," I said.

"I've watched enough about it on television, haven't I? I don't think it ought to be too difficult. Let's have some sherry."

I got up and fetched glasses and a bottle.

As I poured out the sherry, he asked, "What's for supper?"

"Lentil soup and macaroni cheese," I answered.

"Good, I like that." He had admirably simple tastes in food, which was fortunate, considering the state of our finances. He never expected me to provide him with the kind of fare with which I supplied my clients. "Was that Beryl I heard down here?"

"Yes."

"What did she want?"

I told him about the birthday party for Henrietta.

"Nice idea," he said, "but who's going to pay for it?"

"D'you know, I never thought of asking about that," I said. "Beryl said she'd supply the drinks, and I suppose I took for granted she meant to pay for the meal as she was ordering it. But perhaps it ought to be our contribution to the festivities."

"I hate the idea of treating that bastard Martin to anything," Peter said. "He's a mean devil. D'you think he'll really come, or will he find some absolutely unassailable excuse for putting it off at the last minute?"

"I don't know. Will he? You know him better than I do."

"The funny thing is, I don't really know him at all." Sipping some sherry, Peter gazed into the fire, the flames lighting flickering reflections in his blue eyes. "I'd a sort of hero worship of him when I was a kid, then I caught on to the fact that that charm of his didn't mean a thing and that, in fact, he'd no time for me. Surprising, looking back, how much it hurt. Of course, I put it down to his resenting having a stepmother and a half-brother and sister, and to this day I don't know if that's what the trouble was, or if it was simply that he's never had time for anyone who isn't going to be useful to him. But perhaps it's just envy that makes me say that sort of thing. If I'm ever half as successful as he is, I may settle down to putting up with him as he is."

"For Henrietta's sake, I hope he'll come," I said. "It would really please her."

*

That was what I said again a few days later when I happened to meet Grace Kenworthy in Alcaster. I had gone into the town to order a turkey and its attendant trimmings for Henrietta's luncheon, having come to the conclusion that something traditional would please the old woman more than anything more elaborate. I wanted to make sure too that fresh prawns would be available for the prawns in aspic with which I intended the meal to begin, and it was as I was coming out of the fishmonger's that I came face to face with Grace, who was carrying two library books and a shopping basket.

At Grace's suggestion we went into Madeleine's, the little cafe in Alcaster's new shopping centre, for a quick coffee together.

"I haven't got long," she said. "I want to change my books and lay in a few basic supplies for when the family arrive. They needn't expect me to do much in the way of entertaining them. I'll get their rooms ready and give them all breakfast in bed because I hate having to be sociable over my coffee and my *Times,* but I'm going to make it plain they needn't expect anything more from me. I'm much too busy."

Grace was always busy, but, in fact, was not as inhospitable as she sounded. The chances were that she would enjoy having her brothers and her sister-in-law to stay and would go to a good deal of trouble cooking for them and looking after them. She was a sturdy, wide-hipped woman of fifty-two, handsome in a heavy-featured way, with short, straight grey hair, level dark eyebrows that almost met above her nose, and slightly fierce dark eyes. She was wearing a thick tweed suit of a tartan that made her look even broader than she was and a suede jacket.

Striding ahead of me into Madeleine's, she went on in her deep voice, "I'm against this party, you know. Beryl's set her heart on it, so I'm doing what I can to help, but I think it'll be too much for Henrietta. I don't think she cares much for parties, and with her bad heart and all it'll probably wear her out."

"But an eightieth birthday is really an occasion," I said. "I'm glad we're doing something about it. If Martin comes, I think she'll be specially pleased."

We sat down at one of the little round tables and ordered coffee.

"I can't see why she should be," Grace said, "except for the prestige it'll give her to have a celebrity around. He's never troubled to be particularly nice to her. He comes here as seldom as he decently can. I used to think it might be because he resented my father marrying her, yet he was quite fond of Peter and Beryl's mother, and it isn't as if he'd lost financially by father's marrying a third time. The amount he had to leave her, with inflation, was ridiculously small. Sometimes I wonder how she manages. Of course, her first husband left her a certain amount and I know Beryl contributes to everyday expenses. But anyway, Martin has far more money than all the rest of us put together, so, as I said, that can't have anything to do with it. I think it's just the fact that now he's famous he finds us all hopelessly provincial and dull."

"Peter has an idea he may change his mind at the last moment about coming," I said.

"Oh no, he won't do that," Grace said. "I shall see to that."

She looked so formidable as she said it that I thought it would be a daring man who would stand up to her. But then Grace laughed. She had an engaging laugh that brightened her heavy features.

"I'm his older sister, you know, and I believe that to this day he's a little afraid of me. When we were young I used to bully him dreadfully. And he knows he's never succeeded in impressing me quite as much as he'd like to. But I'm really very fond of him and he knows that too, and once or twice, when he's been in trouble, I've been the person he's come to to help him out of it."

"Woman trouble?" I asked.

"What else? Not that he ever takes my advice, which is probably wise of him, but he knows he can say what he likes to me, and the worst I'll do is lecture him as if he weren't grown up yet and hardly knew the facts of life. I think he rather enjoys it. It makes a change from the toadying he's used to."

"I've always had a feeling, from what I've heard of things, that it was the collapse of his marriage that somehow twisted him," I said. "I remember meeting his wife just once. They came down here together when you were all getting the house ready for your father and Henrietta. They were on that trip round the world when they'd just got married. You were decorating the place between you and putting up curtains and pictures and things, and Martin certainly didn't resent Henrietta then, because I can remember him helping. He was on a step-ladder when I saw him, all tangled up in wallpaper and obviously having the time of his life. I thought I'd never seen anyone so handsome."

Our coffee had come. As she stirred a teaspoon of sugar into it, Grace gave a sigh. "And he still is. And unfortunately for me, I resemble him, but what's impressive in a man can be just a bit too much of a good thing in a woman. I was never allowed to have any illusions about my looks. I used to yearn to be a delicate creature like his wife. Louise was really beautiful. You said you saw her."

"Just that once."

"Yes, I remember we took it into our heads to redecorate the place ourselves to save father money. That honeymoon really cost him something, although of course he did a fair amount of lecturing on the way and made a bit of money. Then we had the idea that he and Henrietta were really much too old to be able to cope with a move and that we ought to do as much as we could for them. But naturally when they got back they shifted everything around and got rid of a good deal of their old furniture and bought new things. Still, it was fun doing it. Luke was really very clever at that sort of thing even before he met Vanessa and went into it professionally, and Martin had only just begun to be a success—he was playing Iago in Miles Davidson's *Othello*—and he and Louise were happy. That's to say, he was, because he didn't know Louise was going to walk out on him with that American airline pilot a few days after they got back to London." She was gazing before her into the past with a sort of angry intensity. "I think you're probably right, it was the shock of that that somehow spoiled him. I don't think he's ever had any real emotions since. What a bitch the woman was."

I had heard the whole story before more than once and had always had a certain amount of sympathy with Louise Cosgrove, because Martin, as the whole family agreed, had a vile temper and when his vanity was damaged could be outrageous. His vanity must have suffered greatly when Louise left him, and his heart, supposing he had still had one then, had perhaps been broken, for he had never married again, and he had always been very careful never to be left again, but to do the leaving himself.

He had allowed Louise to divorce him, but whether she

had married her pilot or had adventured further I had never known. I had only a dim memory of her, a willowy blonde with long, shadowy blue eyes and a radiant smile. For me, at ten years old, she had been the perfection of beauty. But by now she must be approaching fifty, and if she was still willowy, must be achieving it by rigid attention to her diet, while the fairness of her hair, if it had not changed colour altogether, no doubt came out of a bottle. But perhaps that had not been her future. Perhaps she had had children, did not bother about her figure and was domesticated and contented and very thankful that twenty years ago she had had the courage to leave the brilliantly handsome but all too temperamental man to whom she had once been married, even though in the end he had turned out to be an exceptionally gifted actor, with a knighthood almost certainly dangling before him.

Grace and I sat over our coffee for half an hour, then Grace set off for the library and I started for home. It was a bright morning, but there had been a heavy frost in the night and the roads were treacherous. I drove slowly along the road to Ickfield. Except for a few lanes that led off it here and there, it ran straight to the crossroads on the edge of the village. If I had taken the turning to the right there, I should have found myself in the heart of it. It was built around a triangular green with a church, two pubs, the excellent and surprisingly sophisticated village shop and some old houses, among them the one where Grace lived, facing on to it. The road to the left led to the Roman villa which was Max Ormerod's passion, and beyond it to an excellent little hotel called The Green Man. But keeping straight on along the road ahead, which suddenly grew narrow after the crossroads, I passed Henrietta's house on the left and only a minute or so later reached my home.

Henrietta's house was one of the oldest in Ickfield. Between the ancient black beams that supported it, it was painted white. The walls leant at what looked impossible angles. There seemed to be no good reason why it should not have tumbled down long ago, yet it had stood firmly where it was for about four centuries. Its roof was thatch and its windows were small and diamond-paned, set in walls a yard thick. When I had been a child, before the Cosgroves had bought it, repaired the thatch and repainted it, I had been faintly afraid of it, feeling that one day some highly sinister old woman might pounce out upon me when I happened to be passing and drag me indoors and bake me in a pie.

In fact, it had been inhabited by the Ormerods, the parents of Max, who were the least frightening of people. When they tempted me inside, it had been to give me Mars Bars or toffees and not to threaten me with being eaten. When old George Ormerod died his widow had sold the house to Professor Cosgrove and had gone to live in a comfortable bungalow in Henley, near to a married sister. Max, who had still been at school, had gone with her, but later had returned as a very junior member of the staff of the museum in Alcaster and had settled into a boarding-house there, where he had remained ever since, regarded by his landlady with possessive devotion.

This apparently suited him. I had always thought of him as an essentially solitary man, though he seemed friendly enough to Peter and me and often sought our company, perhaps specially that of Peter, who had a knack of forming good relationships with the unlikeliest people, from quiet, elusive characters like Max to noisily violent people whom he had met in Alcaster's more disreputable pubs. This could have the appearance of an almost Christian tolerance. Yet if half the people who had confided in him because of what they took for warm sympathy with them had ever read his books, they would have become astonishingly uneasy at encountering the distortions of their own characters that flitted through them.

Driving on past Henrietta's house towards the cottage, I

saw a figure plodding along the road ahead whom I recognized at once and at sight of whom my heart sank. It was Simon Edge, one of Peter's friends whom I really did not like. He was a shabby, unsuccessful artist whom Peter had known since his early days as a journalist when he had been next to penniless himself, and to whom he had remained loyal ever since. Simon had started in his youth in advertizing, but now lived mostly on unemployment benefit, though he occasionally picked up an odd job doing a book jacket or illustrating children's books. In my view he had very little talent, though he could be insufferably pretentious about his work. But what specially dismayed me about seeing him today, walking along the road with dragging footsteps, with a large rucksack on his back, was my knowledge that he descended on Peter and me only when he had really run out of money and that he would expect to be able to stay with us, perhaps for weeks, feeling naïvely certain of his welcome.

Not that he was any trouble when he stayed with us. He was helpful about the house, borrowed only small amounts of money so that he could take us out for drinks in one of the local pubs, and had a way of taking long walks by himself in the evenings, when he communed with his private demons and left Peter and me to ourselves. That, in my view, was his one redeeming quality. He might be lazy and parasitical, but at least you could count on him to keep out of your way every day for two or three hours.

However, in spite of my feelings about him, I pulled the car up alongside him, rolled down the window and said, "Hallo, Simon—want a lift?"

He answered with a delighted smile. He had a very wide smile in a small, monkey-like face. It was mud-coloured and prematurely wrinkled, far more so than Peter's, though they were about the same age. His brown hair was dirty and tangled. But he had large, beautiful grey eyes which sometimes could make you forget how unattractive the rest of him was. He was a small man with wide shoulders and short, slightly bandy legs. Today he was wearing dirty blue jeans and a black leather jacket. The rucksack that he was carrying, which made him look humpbacked, probably contained all that he possessed in the world.

"Freda—lovely!" he exclaimed. "Though we're almost there, aren't we? But still, wonderful to rest my feet." He climbed into the car as I opened the door for him and kissed me warmly and rather moistly. "I've walked from the station. I found there wasn't another bus to Ickfield for two hours, so I thought I might as well get going on my own. A lovely day, anyway. I like this kind of weather. Exhilarating. And the colours at this time of year mean much more to me than all those awful greens in the flush of summer. These lovely browns, the colours of dog shit. Glorious. I don't know why I don't live in the country like you and Peter."

"You're coming to stay with us, I suppose," I said without enthusiasm.

"If that's all right. It *is* all right, I hope?" His tone was anxious. "I tried phoning you yesterday evening to ask if I could come, but there wasn't any answer."

"We were in all yesterday evening," I said. "The phone didn't ring."

I did not believe for a moment that he had tried to telephone us. He knew how easy it is to put a person off on the telephone.

"Must have been something wrong with the line," he said. "I tried several times. If it's inconvenient, of course I'll go to that place, The Green Man. I just had the feeling yesterday I hadn't had a really good natter with Peter for a very long time and that it was just what I needed. If I've hit on a bad time though, just tell me."

He knew that I would not tell him so, and I knew that he could not possibly afford to stay at The Green Man.

"It's all right," I said. "But Peter's working. You mustn't disturb him."

"You know I never do that."

It was true, he did not, or only rarely. There were times when, with a bottle of whisky beside him, he would start on a strange monologue about the evils of life, which might continue until one in the morning, but mostly he was self-contained and unobtrusive and seemed to enjoy the fact that Peter and I left him to himself as much as we were grateful that he did not intrude on us. He seemed to come to us for the sake of a little peace, and I sometimes felt guilty when I realized how much I grudged responding to such a modest demand.

When I took him into the cottage Peter was at work upstairs, but hearing us come in, he came downstairs and seeing Simon, gave him the casual sort of greeting that the two of them were in the habit of giving one another, even if they had not met for a year or two. Then Peter wanted to know what there was for lunch. As there was never anything for lunch but sandwiches of some kind, the question came simply from habit. I answered that today there would be egg and tomato, and after I had taken Simon upstairs to the small spare bedroom that just accommodated a single bed, went to the kitchen to hard-boil some eggs. When I came back to the living-room, leaving the eggs simmering, I found Peter and Simon sitting on either side of the fire, drinking beer. As I fetched sherry for myself, I heard Simon ask Peter how Max Ormerod was.

"All right, I think," Peter said. "I'd forgotten you knew him."

"I met him once when I was here," Simon said. "Nice chap. Dedicated. I like that. He made an impression on me. Still in the same old job, I suppose. I wonder why he's never made it to one of the more important museums. No ambition, is that it? That's good. There's a hell of a lot too much ambition around nowadays, at the expense of the things that give you real satisfaction. You're ambitious, Peter, of course. You keep on hoping you'll take off in a big way one day. Well, good luck to you, though I'll probably like you less when it happens. But I see it must be tantalizing for you, having a major sort of success in the family. Must stimulate competitiveness. I can understand that. Incidentally, the chap can't really act at all, can he? He's simply himself in everything he does. Not what I'd call a real artist."

"I think he's pretty good," Peter said brusquely. He never allowed anyone outside the family to criticize Martin.

"I met Grace in Alcaster this morning," I said. "She said Martin'd definitely be coming for the birthday."

"Whose birthday is this?" Simon asked.

"Henrietta's—my stepmother's," Peter said. "She'll be eighty next Wednesday."

"The old woman who lives in the house up the lane?"

Peter nodded.

"I hope I don't live to be eighty," Simon said. "Artists should die young."

"You'll hang on as long as you can when the time comes," Peter said. "And you're rather past your first youth already. You've put off dying a bit too long for a picturesque early death. Anyway, Henrietta still gets a great deal out of life. She can still drive a car and she gardens and she has plenty of friends. I should think she'll make ninety."

"But Grace thinks this party may be too much for her," I said. "After all, she had that heart attack last year."

"Grace always likes to throw cold water on things," Peter said. "Actually, I think Henrietta's sure to enjoy it, and after all, it's only family, not a great mob of people."

"Family," Simon said. "That's to say, all the people who might benefit by her death suddenly descending on the poor old soul with a bad heart and hoping the strain may knock her out. What you might call a gathering of the vultures."

"You do say the most horrible things, Simon," I said. "It isn't like that at all." I stood up to return to the kitchen to attend to the eggs. "Anyway, Henrietta's got hardly anything to leave. No one will benefit when she dies. Apart from that, we're all very fond of her."

"Hasn't she got some Francis Buller paintings?" Simon asked. "I seem to remember you telling me so. You know he's come into fashion lately. Collectors are after him. If she's really got some, she may be a far richer woman than you realize."

CHAPTER 2

The Francis Buller paintings to which Simon referred were
two landscapes which Henrietta had bought about three
years ago, largely because in one of them her own house
appeared and in the other a corner of the village green of
Ickfield, which showed the church with its square Norman
tower and the old yew tree in the churchyard. Max Ormerod had found the pictures in an antique shop somewhere, had at once recognized the house and the church,
had bought them for what he had said had even then been
a good deal less than their value and later had offered them
to Henrietta because she had let him see how much they
charmed her. She had paid him four hundred pounds for
the two, which was what he had told her he had paid for
them.

I had never cared for them much. Buller, who was
known to have lived in Alcaster for a time and had painted
a good many local scenes, had lived a little too late in the
nineteenth century to appeal to me. He had been affected
already by the beginnings of the pre-Raphaelite movement,
which I had never liked, though I knew vaguely that this
had recently come back into fashion.

"When you say Buller's gone up in value," I said, "do
you mean by hundreds or thousands? The art market seems
to be so crazy nowadays, one can't guess."

"Thousands, thousands!" Simon exclaimed. "One of his
paintings went for over ten thousand at Sotheby's a few
weeks ago. I haven't seen the ones your stepmother's got,
but if they're anything like as good as that one, she's got

herself a nice little nest-egg. Not that he'll ever go into the really high figures, but she's probably made an excellent investment. How long ago did she buy them?"

Peter told him that it was about three years.

"Ah yes. He hadn't really been discovered yet. But a few discerning people had already started to collect him, especially his Alcaster paintings, and that always forces prices up. She got them from Ormerod, I think you once told me. If I were him, I'd be biting my nails now at having let them go."

I went out to the kitchen, put the hard-boiled eggs into cold water and set about making the sandwiches for lunch. I wondered if Simon was speaking the truth about the value of the Francis Buller paintings. That was by no means certain. Simon liked to be thought knowledgeable about the art world and to convey the impression to Peter and me that, impoverished though he might be, he lived at its hub and knew what was happening from day to day while we were mere provincials. I had no direct evidence that he lied to us, but I could not help feeling that a good deal of what he told us sounded as if he were making it up as he went along.

All the same, I thought, it was possible that someone ought to speak to Henrietta about the Buller paintings, to make sure that they were adequately insured. Henrietta was an acute woman in her way, who quite likely had thought of this for herself, but she might not have kept abreast of how sharply Buller prices had risen.

As it turned out, however, there was no need to raise the matter with her. On the morning of her birthday party the rest of the Cosgrove family had assembled by the time Peter and I arrived with the van, with the prawns in aspic, the roast turkey with chestnut stuffing and the birthday cake to follow. We had left Simon behind in the kitchen, contentedly making an omelet for himself. Of course we had not been able to take him to the party with us since Beryl had made it so clear from the start that it was to be strictly family. He had really been very little trouble during the time he had been with us. He had spent a good deal of his time reading and as usual had gone for long walks in the evening, especially enjoying, as he had said, the colours of the deepening twilight and what he called the sheer drama of walking all alone through darkness, in which he claimed to be able to see as well as he could by daylight. He had said nothing about how long he intended to stay, but I was fairly sure it would be at least until after Christmas.

Peter, who was driving the van, took it round to the back door of Henrietta's house, where Beryl ran out to meet us and help us to unload what we had brought. The day was sunny and mild and there were even a few late roses in the garden. Beryl told us that the table in the dining-room was laid and that Henrietta now knew we were coming. She had caught Beryl extending the table to its full length with the two spare leaves which she and Henrietta never used for themselves, and after that it had been impossible to keep the party a secret any longer. But this had happened only just before Grace and the other Cosgroves arrived, so it had been the surprise for Henrietta on which Beryl had set her heart.

I was putting the hot food into the plate-warming drawer of the cooking stove when Henrietta, who had heard the van arrive, trotted out to the kitchen.

"My dears, how sweet of you to go to all this trouble for me," she said, kissing Peter and me. "I've been doing my best to forget I'd a birthday coming. At my time of life that's the best way to treat them. But between you all, you're really making it a treat for once for me to remember it."

She was a small woman who had always been slender and who in her old age had shrunk a little, so that she had become angular where not long ago she had still had curves. But who was as straight as she had ever been and still had neat ankles, of which she was justifiably proud, always wearing good shoes to set them off. She had a small face with a narrow, high-bridged nose and a sharp chin, grey eyes that required glasses only for reading, and a mouth that had grown thin-lipped with age, but was still gently whimsical. Her hair was white, but thick and curly.

"Of course, if I'd known you were all coming, I'd have dressed for the occasion," she went on. "Here I am in my old blouse and skirt and all of you looking so smart. I ought to have guessed there was something up when Beryl put on her new two-piece this morning and didn't go to work. She said she wasn't going because she thought she had a migraine coming on, but you don't put on your newest dress when you're getting a migraine. But I didn't think of it. I'm not as observant as I used to be. And it happened I'd other things on my mind, but I'll tell you about that presently."

Her blouse and skirt, both of a soft lavender shade that suited her, might be old, but she looked very trim in them. Beryl's new two-piece was dark green, which went well with her reddish hair. I had put on a jersey dress of coral-colour and Peter had been coaxed into his one good suit which he could normally be cajoled into wearing only when he had been invited to drinks by some of our more elderly acquaintances in the village, who might be put out if he appeared in a sweater and corduroys. His hair, luckily, was at the stage when it was neither too short nor too long, and he was looking, I thought, remarkably handsome.

But even I, deeply though I loved him, could not persuade myself that he was as handsome as his half-brother Martin who was in the drawing-room with the other Cosgroves when Henrietta took Peter and me in. As Grace had said, she bore a marked resemblance to Martin, but the features that in her looked merely heavy, in him gave an impression of quiet power. The straight dark eyebrows that

almost met above his nose, did not, as with her, give him a
slightly threatening look, but rather one of thoughtfulness
and strength. He was of medium height and rather stocky,
but somehow on the stage he always seemed to look taller
than he was. His eyes were dark and deep-set, like Grace's,
but although he was only two years younger than she, his
dark hair had not started to turn grey. He was wearing a
plum-coloured shirt with a matching tie and light brown
tweeds. At a glance it was easy to see that he was a man
who had made a success of his life and who, without ap-
pearing to make any effort to do so, managed to dominate
everyone else in the room.

Yet his brother Luke was not an insignificant man. He
was the youngest of the first Cosgrove family and not
unlike Grace and Martin, but he was taller and slimmer
than either and though his features were basically of the
same cast as theirs, they were far more finely modelled. He
was fairer too, with straight hair which he wore rather long
but carefully cut, and he had light grey eyes instead of
their smouldering dark ones. He had not their appearance
of force, but had a lazy sort of grace.

His wife, who was forty-five, the same age as Luke, was
a small woman who tended not to be noticed in the company of the Cosgroves until she chose to enter the conversation. Then all of them, perhaps without even being aware
that they did so, grew quiet to take notice of what she had
to say in her serious, emphatic voice. She had smooth
brown hair, a pale, oval face, and she generally wore
black, heavily loaded with jewellery. Today she was in a
black dress that fitted her closely, but had great loose
sleeves which, when they fell back, showed her thin white
wrists and the collection of massive bracelets on them.

Martin greeted me when I came into the room with the
kind of kiss which suggested that he had been waiting
eagerly for this moment, though I felt sure that I had not
been in his thoughts for a moment since he had seen me

last, which was more than a year ago. Yet he had such an air of sincerity that I might have believed in his pleasure if I had not realized long ago that he had the actor's great need to be liked, even by an unimportant audience.

Holding me away from him, he studied me and said, "You're looking terrific. Living with this loon, Peter, seems to agree with you. How are you getting along, Peter? Always scribble, scribble, scribble . . . ? I hope things are going well."

"Tolerably," Peter said, with reserve.

"You must keep going," Martin went on. "I never read anything but thrillers in my spare time. I think yours are jolly good, though a bit too cerebral for my taste. Not enough beatings up and clowning around in bed. That's what I like. Take my advice, put a bit more of that in and your sales will rocket."

"Peter always had a too logical mind," Luke said with the mildly ironic note in his voice which was often there. "He ought to have stuck to mathematics when he was young, instead of blundering into journalism."

"That's right," Martin said. "He's got a cold, clear brain, not a drop of hot blood in him. I don't believe he could describe a scene of real violence, even if he wanted to."

"And I'm very glad he doesn't want to," Henrietta said. "There's so much violence in our daily lives, I don't see why we should have to put up with it in our fiction. With the news telling one every evening about bombing and assassinations and kidnapping and hijackings, I want the murders I read about to be nice, quiet, orderly things, with motives one can understand, instead of the mindless horrors that really happen. Peter, dear, will you pour out our drinks?"

Peter went to the table where the drinks had been set out by Beryl and started pouring them out for everyone while Henrietta sat down in a chair by the fire.

The presents that the Cosgroves had brought her were

into one of his foul moods, you don't force him to understand what he's doing to you."

"So you remember those moods of his, do you?"

"Good Lord, yes. I'm only ten years older than he is, you know, and I lived at home till he was about twelve or thirteen. Even at that age he could cast a gloom over the whole house by going about looking thunderous for no reason anyone could ever understand. He'd never explain it, and then suddenly he'd be back to his normal self, also without explanation. Luckily, he wasn't violent, even at his worst, but he used to drive his mother frantic. Poor Marcia wasn't like Henrietta, who's got incredible strength. Marcia always thought she must be somehow to blame. She was the same with my father, who was the worst of us all. It's from him we inherit our most unattractive qualities."

Though he had lowered his voice, it had a carrying quality and Henrietta, who had been listening to him, suddenly broke in, "How can you say such a thing, Martin? Raymond was the gentlest, most undemanding of men."

"But how cruel you can be by being too gentle and undemanding," he said. "You can give the impression of not really wanting anything or anyone. I can't remember ever feeling that he wanted any of us. All he ever wanted was to be looked after nicely and left alone to go ahead with his work."

"With which I sympathize," she answered. "I think I'm the same kind of person."

"Oh, you're not!" Beryl exclaimed. "If you were, we shouldn't all be so fond of you."

"You're all very good to me," Henrietta said. "You're making this a lovely day for me. And that makes me wonder if it's the right time to talk about something I've got on my mind. Not that I suppose it'll distress you much, and as you're all gathered together here, it'll save me writing round to you. The fact is, I'm thinking of selling my Francis Bullers."

on a table beside her. She had just added to them what Peter and I had brought her, a book of flower prints which we had heard her say that she would like to buy if it were not such a terrible price, and that really it was impossible to go on buying books nowadays. Yet, in fact, that continued to be her one extravagance. The room was lined with book-shelves and had not much else in it but some comfortable, chintz-covered chairs and a few small tables.

It was not a big room, and the dark-beamed ceiling, like all the ceilings in this ancient house, was low and the windows were small, so that the eight people collected there made the room seem crowded. One of the Francis Buller paintings, the one in which this house appeared, hung over the fireplace. The other was in the dining-room.

Going to the table beside Henrietta, I looked at the presents that the others had brought. Grace had brought a quilted bed-jacket of apricot-coloured satin, which she had probably made herself, for she was a highly skilled needlewoman. Martin had brought an amethyst necklace, which had been clever of him, because amethysts were Henrietta's favourite stones. Luke and Vanessa had brought a wrought-iron lamp of curious design, which no doubt would have gone well with the kind of interior decoration they favoured, but which did not look altogether appropriate in the old-fashioned room. Beryl's present was a Chelsea bowl, which she had probably found in an antique shop in Alcaster. The room was full of flowers. They had been brought, Henrietta told me, by Martin. The old woman had more colour in her cheeks than usual and her eyes sparkled. It was difficult to realize that she was eighty.

Over drinks and presently over lunch, Martin took charge of the conversation. He seemed to think this was the best way of making sure that the occasion was a success for Henrietta. Luke was normally a quiet man and did not say much. Beryl had placed me next to Martin at the dining-table. He was on Henrietta's right and Luke on her left. Martin had recently returned from a very successful season in New York and thought that nothing could fascinate his hearers more than an account of his opinions of the New York theatre, New York hotels, New Yorkers and the very little that he knew about the political situation in America.

"But it's always good to get home," he said. "All the same, I sometimes wonder why I don't settle there. I seem to understand them, you know. We get on splendidly. I'm always happy when I'm over there. And yet, as I said, it's good to get home. Don't ask me why. My home is a three-room flat, where my roots go about three inches into the soil, or rather the concrete. You don't know how I envy people who have real roots, like you, Henrietta. It must be wonderful to have an old house like this and a real sense of belonging here."

"The funny thing is, I don't feel in the least that I belong here," Henrietta said. "I've only lived here twenty years and at my age twenty years is gone in a flash. I'm still very aware of the people who lived here before me, the Ormerods, for instance. D'you know, when Max comes to see me, I sometimes have the feeling that he has more right to live here than I have. And before the Ormerods, who lived here only fifteen years or so, there were some people called Smith, I believe, and before them, heaven knows who. The truth is, very few people have roots anywhere nowadays. We've got to learn to live without them, and I don't think we've completely reconciled ourselves to the fact. There's something in human nature that craves for them. I was born in London, but I've lived in Manchester, Sheffield, Nairobi, Adelaide and Glasgow. Ickfield sometimes seems just another brief stopping-place on the way to the tomb."

"I don't want to be put into a tomb," Vanessa said abruptly. "I can't bear the thought. I've left clear instructions in my will that I'm to be cremated and my ashes scattered in the Thames from Battersea Bridge. I think that's a

good place for it. No one would notice it being done. You wouldn't get into trouble for dropping litter. I don't want to be any trouble to anyone."

Her earnest, incisive voice, unlike the lightness of Henrietta's, had the effect that it so often had of creating silence. All of us round the table had an uncomfortable feeling that she was talking about death in all seriousness, which was not the right subject for the birthday party of someone who was eighty years old.

*

To break the silence, I said, "I've lived in Ickfield nearly all my life and even in the same house. Am I unique?"

Martin turned to look at me, his deep-set eyes studying me thoughtfully. Dropping his voice, so that what he said seemed to be only for me, while the others could talk about something else, he said, "Very nearly, I think. Henrietta's right, we've all got used to living in a state of perpetual motion. But this is what you like, is it? You're happy?"

He had the art of making it sound as if it really mattered to him to know how one would answer. But it was embarrassing, I thought, to be asked if one was happy, because even when perhaps one was, one was hardly ever aware of the fact. It was only later that one looked back and said to oneself, "How happy I was then."

"Oh yes," I said, "it suits me very well. But I'm not sure how much longer it's going to go on suiting Peter. I should think it might be useful to a writer to migrate from time to time. Perhaps we'll go to France, or Spain, or somewhere more colourful than Ickfield."

"Don't let him make you go if you don't want to," Martin said. "We Cosgroves have a way of taking it out of our women. You shouldn't let us do it."

"So it's our fault, is it?"

"Partly, yes. It would be for our good if you'd stand up to us. You don't stand up to Peter, do you? When he ge

There was a brief silence and for a moment the eyes of everyone there turned to the picture that hung over the fireplace. It was the painting of Ickfield church, with the old yew tree in the foreground.

Then Luke said, "I think that's a pretty wise step, Henrietta. The market's just right for it. He's in fashion at the moment, but it may not last. It's not as if he's a genuinely outstanding painter. Have you a buyer in mind?"

"I have, as a matter of fact," she said. "A Mr. Everett Baynes, an American who's been collecting Bullers for the last few years, specially his Alcaster paintings, and who's partly responsible by doing that, so I understand, for the way the prices have shot up. He's coming to take a look at my pictures tomorrow, and if he likes them, he's ready to buy them."

"Tomorrow!" Beryl cried in a shrill voice. "You haven't said a word about this to me."

Henrietta leant back in her chair. The table had been almost cleared by then of everything but the birthday cake, which she had cut, after blowing out the single candle and telling us all that she had made a wish. We were drinking coffee.

"I didn't want to worry you till I knew where I was," she said. "It's Max who told me I might get seven or eight thousand for each of them, but perhaps he's quite wrong. I don't think he knows a great deal about that kind of thing and he could be mistaken. I shan't sell them unless I get a good price."

Martin leant forward and gently took hold of one of her hands.

"Henrietta, what you're really telling us is that you're very hard up and need the money. That's what you didn't want us to worry about."

She gave an apologetic smile. "Well, yes, I'm certainly finding things a bit tight. You see, Raymond and my first husband too both retired when university pensions still came in the form of a lump sum which you could invest as you saw fit. Quite a generous sum it sounded at the time. Now I believe the system's quite different. You get a much smaller lump sum than we did, but you get an index-linked pension for the rest of your life, so you don't run into the kind of difficulties I have. First of all, you see, when I inherited the money I did from each of my husbands, there were still death duties on what you inherited from a spouse. That's been changed since, but of course in those days it took quite a slice of my capital. I put that capital into an annuity, which seemed more than adequate at the time, but now, what with inflation, it doesn't amount to much. So it's true that at the moment I'm rather hard up and that the sale of the pictures, sad as I am to think of it, would help for a time. Perhaps for as long as I'll need. And I don't think the pictures mean very much to any of you. They don't, do they? It wouldn't distress you if they went out of the family?"

"Damn the pictures!" Martin exclaimed. "Why haven't you told us any of this before?"

"Yes, why have you never said anything about it to me?" Beryl asked. "I could easily have paid you more for my keep than I've been doing."

"You pay me more than you should already," Henrietta said. "As much as you can possibly afford. I wouldn't dream of letting you give me any more."

Vanessa put her elbows on the table, her sleeves falling back and her bracelets jangling.

"You've one asset, Henrietta, you haven't mentioned," she said. "This house. You'd get at least seventy or eighty thousand for it, perhaps more, anyway far more than your Mr. Baynes will pay you for the pictures."

"Vanessa!" It was Martin, and he sounded angry. "This is Henrietta's home. In God's name, how can you suggest such a thing?"

"But she was saying only a few minutes ago that even

after all these years, she doesn't feel she has roots here," Vanessa said in her calm, reasonable way. "And the house is ever so much larger than she needs, and she must find the stairs quite trying, they're so steep, and she'd really be far more comfortable in a small modern bungalow, all on one floor. I've decided that when I'm old I'm going to move into the smallest bungalow I can find, with every possible comfort laid on. I've given the matter some thought. I dislike the idea of going to live in an old people's home, even a very luxurious one. I want to keep my independence as long as I can, but I can't see the virtue of clinging to something large and old and inconvenient when one's past being able to enjoy it."

"And where are you going to put Luke in this bungalow of yours?" Martin asked. "In the attic?"

"Oh, that's all right," Luke said easily. "She's decided she's going to survive me, and I agree with her, she probably will. I hope so, anyway. I'll still have a devoted wife to look after me when I'm senile. What she does after I die is up to her."

"My dears, my dears!" Henrietta cried. "What nonsense you're talking! You're all quite young. Oh, I know you're what's called middle-aged, but to me that's young. You shouldn't be thinking about this kind of thing at all yet."

"But I think one should," Vanessa said earnestly. "The increasing number of people surviving into old age is becoming one of our most pressing social problems. And as I said, I've given it a great deal of thought, because I don't want to be overtaken by it suddenly when I'm past coping. Believe me, Henrietta, you would be wise to sell this house quite soon, buy another annuity with what you get for it, and move into something small and convenient and much cheaper to run than this. And closer to shops, of course, so that it won't matter to you so much when you can't drive any longer."

Martin's face had turned a dusky red. "You appalling

woman, shut your mouth!" he snarled. "I just said, this is
Henrietta's home, and if I have any say in the matter, no
one's going to shift her out of it into some beastly bungalow." He swung round on Grace. "Don't you agree with
me?"

"Of course I do," she said, but there was a shade of anxiety on her face. It was possible, I thought, that Grace was
afraid that if Henrietta ever gave up her home, Grace herself might be expected to take her in and look after her. If
she had to, she would probably do it without complaint, for
she had a strong sense of duty, but fond of Henrietta as she
appeared to be, taking care of an aged woman might be
something that she would not look forward to with any
eagerness.

"You're happy here, aren't you, Henrietta?" Grace went
on. "You don't want to move?"

"Of course she doesn't," Luke said. "It's just that
Vanessa likes organizing things. She organizes me from
morning to night. It suits me. It saves me a lot of wear and
tear. But Henrietta may not welcome it as I do."

"Well, for God's sake, make the damned woman shut
up!" Martin said disgustedly. "I don't like this talk of old
age and death. Can't you see how it's upsetting Henrietta?"

But Henrietta was laughing again.

"None of you need worry," she said. "I haven't the
slightest intention of selling the house. Of course,
Vanessa's right, it would be the sensible thing to do, but I
simply couldn't face the thought of the upheaval."

"That's what I thought," Martin said. "I know it would
be much too much for you. It's much more sensible to stay
where you are."

"Yes, a move's so upsetting at any time," Grace said.
"Going through all the rubbish one's accumulated over the
years and throwing the wrong things away—I dread the
thought I may have to do it myself sometime."

"I agree," Luke said. "One's rubbish is precious. One

should not be forced to discard it, which happens inevitably if one moves from a big house into a small one."

Peter was watching Henrietta with a worried frown. "All the same, Henrietta, if money's tight, this house is your best asset. Perhaps you ought to think over what Vanessa said."

"Not on your life!" Martin said. "No, what we obviously ought to do is to make Henrietta's income up to something reasonable between us. I'm sure you all agree with me."

"Of course," Grace said. "If only we'd understood the situation before, we could have done it long ago."

"Just so," Luke said.

Martin looked at Peter. "And what about you?"

I knew that Peter could do nothing but agree to join in with the others, though I wondered where the money was to come from.

But before he could answer Henrietta said quietly, "Do let's stop this. I wish I hadn't started it. I don't want anything from any of you. I'm very grateful to you all for being so generous, I truly am, but I'll just sell my Bullers and do very nicely. There's only one thing more I want to say. As I told you, I've used my capital to buy an annuity and that will stop when I die, but the house will remain and I think you should know I've left it in my will to Beryl. It's her home as much as it's mine, and she'll never earn very much in that job she loves so much, not nearly so much as the rest of you, so I think I owe it to her. Besides that, she's done so much for me all these years that I want to show her how grateful I am and how much I love her. I hope none of you will feel I don't care about you because I haven't left you anything."

"Oh darling, you shouldn't . . ." Beryl began in a choked voice, then put her hands to her eyes and did not say any more.

Martin smiled. "I'm sure we all feel it's the best thing you could possibly do, Henrietta. But my prophesy is it'll be years before Beryl comes into her inheritance. I can see us all, looking a good deal more worn than we do now and with a lot more grey hairs, assembling for your ninetieth birthday."

"Make it my hundredth, while you're at it," she answered gaily. She stood up. Her cheeks were faintly flushed and her eyes very bright, signs that in spite of her liveliness she was beginning to feel tired. "You're all invited. Now let's go through to the drawing-room and please don't worry about clearing up in here. Beryl and I will see to it later."

But Beryl and I began to clear up as soon as the others were settled in the drawing-room. They did not stay much longer. Grace had noticed the signs of fatigue in Henrietta and soon collected her brothers and Vanessa to return to her home in the village. They drove away in Martin's Bentley, in which they had come. Peter came out to the kitchen to help with the washing up and with stacking our pots and pans in the van, while Henrietta went upstairs to lie down. It was about four o'clock and dusk already when Peter and I returned to the cottage.

Simon was just about to set out for his evening walk when we got in. He asked how the party had gone, was interested to hear that Everett Baynes was coming to look at the Bullers, said that he hoped Henrietta would get a good price for them, then left Peter and me to ourselves. He had let the fire get low, but Peter stoked it up and for a while we sat quietly beside it, waiting for the sense of anticlimax that follows a party to wear off. Neither of us felt like doing anything and we did not talk much. Peter looked abstracted and presently went upstairs to his room and his typewriter began to tap. But it did not go on for long. Silence soon settled in.

I stayed by the fire, beginning to feel drowsy, thinking that I ought to go out to unload the van and put the dishes into the dishwasher, but I did not want to move. I thought dreamily about the fact that Peter seemed to be quite wrong about his half-brother, Martin. Peter had called him mean. Yet Martin had been the one who had suggested that all the Cosgroves should join together to provide Henrietta with a comfortable income. Peter might say that Martin, with his knowledge of Henrietta, had known that she would refuse his offer and that he had only been making a gesture that had cost him nothing. Yet I had a feeling that Martin had been sincere. He had certainly been genuinely upset at the thought that Henrietta might be driven to leave her home. I began to think that Peter might be somewhat mistaken about Martin's character.

Somewhere in the midst of this musing, I lost track of my thoughts and drifted off to sleep.

It was the sound of the typewriter overhead beginning to tap again that wakened me and I looked at my watch and saw that I must have been asleep for at least an hour. The fire had burned low and needed to have a log or two added to it. I bent forwards to reach for the logs, then paused. There was a curious smell in the air, a smell of smoke, and it did not come from the hearth before me.

My first thought was that I must have left something on the kitchen stove and that it was burning. Yet at the same time I knew that that was not right. I knew that I had left nothing there. All the same, it was my first instinctive action to leap up and make a dash towards the kitchen. But in doing so, I passed one of the living-room windows and saw that the sky outside was the wrong colour. Instead of unbroken darkness, there was an angry copper light in the sky. As I stood still, staring, I realized how strong the smell of burning was. Then my sleep-drugged mind cleared and I understood what was happening.

I sprang to the bottom of the stairs.

"Peter!" I shouted. "Peter—come! Henrietta's house is on fire!"

CHAPTER 3

Peter came down the stairs in a few bounds and raced out of the house. I followed him, but was soon far behind him. In the light of the fire I could see his tall, thin figure as he ran up the lane ahead of me, trailing a long, grotesque shadow behind him. The air was full of the stench of burning and a roaring sound. Above the blaze of the house I saw sparks leaping high in the air. When I was near enough to see more, I saw it was the thatched roof that was on fire, but that the flames were spreading rapidly to engulf the lower part of the old house, which was built so much of wood that it would be consumed in no time.

Terrible anxiety for Henrietta and for Beryl filled me. Death by fire seemed to me one of the most fearful deaths there could be, and I dreaded seeing what seemed sure to be waiting for me when I reached the gate. As I came nearer, heat swept over me, and all the time there was the horrible smell, which seemed to drench me and become part of me.

Peter had disappeared into the garden before I reached it, leaving the gate open behind him. As I went through it, Beryl staggered out of the house by the front door. Smoke billowed out around her. There were sparks smouldering on her dress and she was coughing convulsively. She blundered straight into Peter before she became aware of him as he seized hold of her and began to beat at the sparks on her dress. She dropped her hands then and flung one pointing at the house.

"Do something, do something!" she shrieked, then began

coughing again, retching dreadfully and bending nearly double.

But already someone else was doing something. At first, in the sudden glare from a new burst of flame out of what had been a patch of black shadow, I could not make out who it was, but I saw a slight figure come running from an outhouse, carrying a ladder. As soon as Peter saw him, he went to help. It was Max Ormerod. He and Peter propped the ladder against a window at which, I suddenly saw, Henrietta was standing waiting. There was a red light behind her, as if there was already fire in her room, but she stood quite still. But as soon as the ladder was lodged firmly against the window sill, she opened the window calmly and began to climb out.

With the opening of the window, smoke poured out of it and for a moment she and Max, who had climbed the ladder to try to help her, were invisible. Then they emerged under the cloud and I saw Henrietta cautiously feeling her way down the ladder, rung by rung. She was wearing a dressing-gown and slippers. Max went down the ladder just below her, but stayed near enough to her to catch her if she fell. Reaching the ground before she did, he stood waiting and caught her as she quietly collapsed in his arms.

At the same moment flames burst out of the window from which she had escaped. It was the window of her bedroom, in which the ceiling appeared just to have come crashing down.

Max and Peter carried her a little way from the house and laid her down on a paved path there.

"I've a coat in my car," Max said, and went running off to fetch it.

The car was in the lane, just outside the gate. I had been vaguely aware of it there when I arrived, but had given no thought to whose it was. Max came back in a moment, carrying a coat and as Henrietta sat up and began trying to get to her feet, he wrapped it round her. She croaked out thanks, her voice hoarse, as if she had smoke in her lungs, but already her face had lost the vacant look of shock that it had had at first. Beryl knelt beside her and put her arms round her.

"I tried to get to you," she said, her voice shaking, "but I couldn't get up the stairs. I was in the kitchen when it started—I smelt it, but I didn't realize it was us, I thought it was a bonfire somewhere, or something in the road—and when I realized, I tried to get up the stairs, but I couldn't. I did try, Henrietta."

Henrietta patted her hand. "Of course you did. And I tried to get down the stairs, but I was too late. They were burning already. So I went back to my room and decided if no one came to rescue me, I'd take my chance and jump. It isn't so very high. I might have been all right. And anyway I'd sooner have a broken skull than be roasted alive. But Max came—God bless you, Max."

She gave him a smile that was only a little more tremulous than one of her normal ones.

"If you can manage to get into my car," he said, "I could take you along to Peter's cottage." He looked at Peter. "Isn't that the best thing to do?"

Max was five years younger than Peter, a few inches shorter and was almost as thin, with a slight stoop and a jerky, slouching way of moving. He had a mobile, sensitive face, already marked with more lines than seemed right for his age and which sometimes twitched sharply if he was in a nervous mood. But nervous or not, he had climbed the ladder without showing any fear of the fire. It occurred to me that he might be the stuff of which heroes are sometimes made, the kind of people who are deeply afraid of human relationships, and sometimes even of eating something which they think will disagree with them, but will calmly defuse a bomb. His hair was fair and was already showing a bald patch at the back and he wore glasses over his short-sighted blue eyes.

Peter agreed. "Can you walk to the car, Henrietta, or shall Max and I carry you?"

"Oh, I can walk," she said, "if you'll just help me up. I always find it a little difficult to get up again if I get into this sort of position. But the house . . ." Her voice broke. "The fire-brigade . . . have you sent for them? . . . Oughtn't I to wait? I'm not sure I ought to go away."

"There's nothing you can do here," Peter said, "and I'm sure you ought to get indoors. If you'll go home with Freda, I'll wait here for the fire-brigade, though they'll be too late to be able to save anything."

"But they've been sent for, haven't they?" Henrietta looked at Beryl. "Did you get to the telephone? No, of course you didn't. How could you? So perhaps they aren't even coming. But you're quite right, Peter, they'd be too late to help."

Peter and Max had raised her to her feet, but she did not cling to them. Huddling Max's coat around her, she stood still, watching her old home go up in flames. Other people had started to arrive and were crowding in at the gate. They had seen the blaze from the village and though perhaps in the first instance they had come to see if they could help, they stayed merely to stare, seeing that there was nothing to be done. Most of the faces showed excitement at the spectacle before them, though some looked solemn and awe-struck at the sight of such destruction.

One of the excited faces in the crowd was that of Simon Edge. I had not seen him arrive, but there he was, with his eyes glistening and his mouth slightly open and seeming to be breathing rapidly in what was clearly intense enjoyment. I had heard that fires could move people deeply with a pleasure that was almost sexual, and that was what I thought I saw on Simon's face.

Just as the siren of the fire-engine could first be heard, Grace, Martin, Luke and Vanessa arrived. Though Beryl had not been able to telephone, someone in the village must have sent for the Alcaster fire-brigade. The crowd parted to let in the fire-engine, which was closely followed by another. In seconds, it seemed, men had leapt off them, with long streamers of hoses trailing behind them, to wage what was certainly a hopeless battle.

Grace came running to Henrietta and threw her arms round her.

"You got out!" she cried. "Oh God, I was so frightened when we realized the blaze was here. We just smelt it, you know, and when we saw the light in the sky we somehow couldn't really believe it was this house, even when we knew it couldn't be anywhere else. One's so stupid. But you go out in time—oh God, I'm so thankful!"

"Max got me out," Henrietta said. "He fetched a ladder and put it against my window and helped me down. Beryl managed to get out by herself because she was on the ground floor when it started."

"Where did it start?" Martin asked. He was standing with his hands in his pockets, watching the fire with absorbed interest, and as one of the old walls of lath and plaster, held together by wooden beams, came down with a sudden crash, he drew in his breath sharply, but otherwise he did not move.

"It looks as if it started in the roof," Peter said. "The fire-brigade people may be able to tell. Not that it seems of much importance now."

"It may be when it comes to the question of insurance," Vanessa, the practical one, said. "You were insured, weren't you, Henrietta? I mean, for the real, present-day value of the place, not just for what you paid for it years ago."

"Oh, I think so," Henrietta answered a little uncertainly. "I never quite understood it, but I know my premiums went up every year and the valuation seemed to keep going up too. Oh yes, I think I'm insured. But I can't quite take in that I've lost everything—and Beryl has too. We've neither of us even any clothes left."

She opened Max's coat a little to show that she was in her dressing-gown.

"I think you should come along to the cottage," I said. "I'll find you something to wear."

"Can she and Beryl spend the night with you?" Grace asked. "My spare bedrooms are all taken up. But they could move in with me tomorrow when the others leave. I'll have lots of room then."

I had already been working out how to fit Henrietta and Beryl into the cottage. Simon would have to move out of the little spare bedroom so that Henrietta could sleep there, while he could sleep on the living-room sofa. And there was a chair in Peter's workroom which could be extended into a not too uncomfortable bed on which Beryl could sleep.

"So you'll be doing what I advised after all," Vanessa said, "and end up in a nice little bungalow or flat. I'm sure in the end, when you've got used to it, you'll say the fire was a blessing in disguise."

"Will nothing make that woman keep her mouth shut?" Martin exploded. His vibrant voice carried so far, even in the murmuring of the crowd, the roaring of the flames and the hissing of the powerful jets of water from the house, that heads were turned towards him. "If I were Luke, I'd drown her."

"She's never had much sense of occasion," Luke said mildly, "but she has a dreadful way of being right. Just wait and see."

"Let's go, Henrietta," I said. "Ready, Max?"

He nodded and gave his arm to Henrietta. They started to make their way towards the gate.

"Coming, Beryl?" I asked.

Beryl gave a deep sigh and said, "I suppose I might as well."

Police had already appeared by then and were trying to move the people who had streamed in at the gate out into the lane.

"I'll stay for a bit," Peter said. "The fire people may want to know a few things, as we were the first people on the scene."

Beryl and I followed Max and Henrietta through the crowd and managed to make our way to Max's car. The drive to the cottage took us only two or three minutes.

As he helped Henrietta out of the car, Max said, "I'll drive on home, Freda. There's nothing more I can do here. But you know where to find me if by any chance you should want me."

"Oh, Max—and I've hardly thanked you!" Henrietta cried. "And your coat—here it is! And thank you, thank you! If it weren't for you, I'd be burnt to a crisp by now." She was trying to speak gaily, but her voice was full of emotion.

One side of his face twitched as he gave one of his little nervous smiles.

"I thought you'd decided to jump," he said. "It wasn't so very far. A few broken bones, that's all you'd have had."

"Quite a serious matter at my age," Henrietta replied. "The bones don't always knit. And I hate hospitals. But I think I must have been protected by the wish I made when I blew out the candle on my cake."

"What was that?" I asked. "Beryl told me it would be that she should get married."

"Oh no, it was a much more selfish wish than that," Henrietta said. "It was simply for a painless death. And you were sent to look after me, Max. Thank God you were passing."

He gave her an embarrassed little pat on the arm and shambled off to his car.

I opened the cottage door and led Henrietta and Beryl in.

"He didn't tell us how he came to be passing," Henrietta said. "I wonder what he was doing."

"Oh, he must have been working late at the dig," Beryl said, "and seen the fire from the crossroads."

She was referring to a kind of office that Max had on the site of the Roman villa where he often spent hours alone, particularly in the evenings when his work at the museum was done, fiddling with minute pieces of pottery that had been sifted out of the soil there.

"Yes, that's where he must have come from," I said. I stirred up the smouldering logs in the fireplace. "Now what would you like, some tea or a drink?"

"A drink for me, please," Henrietta said.

"Sweet tea is supposed to be better for shock," I said. "I learnt that once in a first-aid class."

"All the same, a drink, please," Henrietta said. "Whisky, if you've got it. I'm not as shocked as all that."

"Beryl?" I asked.

"Me too—whisky," Beryl answered.

I brought glasses, whisky and a siphon, made drinks for the three of us and we sat down round the fire, Beryl in the new dress that had been singed here and there and Henrietta in her dressing-gown. Under it, I realized, she was fully clothed, except for the blouse and skirt that she had worn earlier in the day. She must have taken them off and put on the dressing-gown when she went upstairs to lie down after her birthday party, but had been meaning to get up and dress again presently when she felt like coming down once more.

"What a tame and friendly thing a fire is in the right place," Henrietta said dreamily, leaning back in her chair, nursing her glass. "Like water, which is so useful and so beautiful and so quiet till it gets out of hand. Fire and flood are the two things I'm really frightened of. I never thought I'd have to endure either in Ickfield."

"But the fact is," Beryl said, "those old houses, lovely as they are, are absolute fire-traps."

"Yes, and I ought to have listened to you long ago and had the place rewired," Henrietta said. "I suppose that was the trouble, a short in the roof."

"It must have been," Beryl said. "There was a trailing mass of flex there, some of it with the insulation actually broken down. Last time I was up there, looking for something, I remember thinking I must talk to you about it, but I forgot."

"I probably shouldn't have done anything about it," Henrietta replied, "Rewiring makes such a horrible mess and sounds so expensive. I knew it ought to be done, but I kept putting it off because I felt I couldn't afford it, just as I did with redecoration of the whole house. I know I let it get dreadfully shabby. But that doesn't matter now." She gave a deep sigh.

"It's just occurred to me," I said, "oughtn't you to let your Mr. Baynes know that there's not much point in his coming tomorrow? Those Bullers he's interested in will have gone up in the holocaust."

"Oh dear, you're quite right," Henrietta said. "We ought to telephone. Could you do that for me, Freda? He's staying at Claridge's. You can get the number from Inquiries, and if he isn't in you can leave a message. And then perhaps, as you said, you could find me something to wear. You're so much taller than I am, it'll trail on the ground, but you're so slim, it probably won't be an awful lot too loose for me. Not that it matters if it is. Isn't it strange, when a real catastrophe happens, one doesn't just worry about the big things that matter, but about quite trivial things too. Everything gets out of proportion. Who's going to care how I look? All the same, I'll feel silly in the morning in a dressing-gown."

"We'll find you something," I said. "And I'll telephone straight away."

It did not take me long to be put in contact with Mr. Everett Baynes at Claridge's. I told him as briefly as I could what had happened. In a kindly American voice he clucked sympathy, stated that for him personally it was a very great disappointment as he had been looking forward so eagerly to adding another two Francis Bullers to his collection, that he had been particularly anxious to do this as he had always specialized in Buller's Alcaster paintings, which represented the artist at the height of his powers, but that if they were gone they were gone. It was a tragedy, but there was nothing more to be said. He thanked me for the courtesy of having taken the trouble to telephone to save him a useless journey next day, when I and my friends must have so much else on our minds, said good night, rang off and passed out of our lives.

As I put the telephone down, I said, "By the way, Henrietta, how did you get in touch with him in the first place?"

"I wrote to him," Henrietta answered. "I read about his buying a Buller at Sotheby's for ten thousand, so I wrote to him, care of them, and had a telephone call in a day or two. Well, it's sad they've gone up in smoke, but I'm beginning to realize there are other things I'm going to miss more, my books, for instance. I'm taking in only little by little what I've actually lost."

"Were the pictures properly insured?" I asked. "I mean, for their present value, not for what you paid for them?"

"No, they weren't. It was only when I read about that sale that I realized how their value had risen, and I didn't even think of reinsuring them because I was expecting to sell them. As I told Vanessa, I think it's all right about the insurance on the house, but the pictures were something a bit special. They ought to have been covered separately. I'm sure the insurance people will argue about their value. Oh dear, one always has to pay for one's stupidity, doesn't one?"

"Well, can you come upstairs to see if we can find you something to wear?" I said. "Or shall I bring a selection down here?"

"Oh, I'll come up," Henrietta said, finishing her whisky and getting to her feet.

"And what about you, Beryl?" I asked.

"I'm all right, thank you," Beryl answered. "If I could just borrow a night-dress or pyjamas or something for to-night and some kind of jacket to go out in in the morning. Then I can go into Alcaster and buy a few things to be going on with. I don't know how long it takes for insurance to come through, but luckily my bank balance is quite healthy at the moment. I'm beginning to think it'll be rather nice to have a completely new outfit. Usually I can't be bothered to buy clothes, even when I get bored with my old things. If you keep them long enough you get to like them again. This two-piece is the first new thing I've bought for ages. It's a pity it's ruined." She made an attempt at a smile.

Leaving her sitting alone by the fire, Henrietta and I went upstairs to see what my wardrobe could offer her.

*

When we came down again, Simon had joined Beryl. I had found a grey jersey for Henrietta, which fitted her quite well, and an old tweed skirt which belonged to a time when hems had been shorter than they were just then, so that it did not look very much too long for her, though it had had to be tightened around the waist with safety-pins. But I had not been able to help with shoes. My feet were far larger than Henrietta's, so she still wore her red velvet slippers.

Simon stood up when we came in and I introduced him to her. He seemed to have been talking excitedly to Beryl. His face was flushed and his eyes, which looked so strangely large and beautiful in his small monkey-face, were brilliant. I wondered for a moment if he had been drinking, but recognized almost at once that it was only his own emotions that had intoxicated him.

"I've just been telling Miss Cosgrove," he said, "I've never in my life seen anything so wonderful. I know I shouldn't say anything of the sort—I know it, I know it, you don't have to tell me—I'm being obscene. But I can't help it. That glorious light and the enormous drama of fire. I beg your pardon, Mrs. Cosgrove, for being revolting, but I can't keep it in. And that thrilling rescue. Superb. The only problem now is how I'm going to be able to survive without having a chance to repeat the experience, because I don't suppose I shall ever have a ringside seat for another splendid fire for the rest of my life."

Henrietta sat down. "You could always become a what d'you call it—a pyromaniac, isn't that the word for it?—and light your own fires. I'm sorry it wasn't you who had to climb down that ladder, Mr. Edge, rather than me. No doubt you would have found that even more dramatic."

"Ah no, it was the watching it that was the supreme thrill," he said. "To *see* it! I don't want to take part in things, you know, I want to *see*. And then, if I can, to paint them. But I know it'll be beyond me to paint what I've seen tonight. The enormous sense of power that fire has! I could never do it."

Henrietta gave him one of her chillier looks. "If you don't mind my saying so, Mr. Edge, you seem to me a rather egocentric young man. The fire was not a pleasant experience for all of us."

"Egocentric—I am, I am, that's just what I am!" he cried, beaming at her. "The perfect word for it. It's what an artist has to be, that's why most of us are so intolerable. But come, be honest, Mrs. Cosgrove, didn't all that colour and heat and that devastating destruction excite you too? Even if you were losing everything you possessed in the world, wasn't it wonderful?"

Beryl suddenly stood up. She looked as if she were thinking of plunging out of the room into the darkness outside, but then slowly she sat down again. She was trembling. Henrietta reached out and put a hand on her arm.

"Don't take it all so much to heart, Beryl," she said. "We'll survive. We'll look for a bungalow, just as Vanessa told us we should, and we'll be just as happy in it as we were in the dear old house. It's just a matter of adjustment. I know it's probably easier for me than for you because really I don't much mind how I end my days as long as I'm comfortable and warm and see a few friends now and then. Possessions don't seem to matter so very much any more. Of course, for you it's different. But perhaps a new home, nearer your work and much easier to look after, will do you all the good in the world, just like that new outfit of clothes you were talking about. Anyway, that's what we should hope."

I spoke quickly because it looked as if Simon was going to break in once more. "Simon, you're going to have to give up your room to Mrs. Cosgrove and sleep on the sofa down here. You can come and help me make up her bed."

"With pleasure," he said. "I can sleep anywhere. On the floor, if need be."

"You're welcome to the sofa," I said. "It's quite comfortable. Now come along."

I hurried him out of the room before he could say anything further to upset Henrietta and Beryl.

Peter returned to the cottage about an hour later. By then I had emptied the van, which I had omitted to do earlier, and had set out a cold supper of ham and salad and cheese. But no one had any appetite except Simon, who ate heartily. But luckily his excitement had simmered down and he had become more silent than usual. He seemed either to be brooding on the glory of the sight that he had seen, trying to fix it in his memory, or else to have some other thoughts on his mind that were occupying him deeply.

Henrietta was showing signs of exhaustion and as soon as supper was over said that she would go to bed. I went upstairs with her to make sure that she had everything she wanted, then, coming down, met Beryl at the foot of the stairs. She was also on her way to bed on the chair in Peter's work-room.

She paused for a moment.

"I don't like your friend Simon," she said.

"I'm sorry about him," I said. "He isn't my favourite person either. But Peter's known him for years and seems attached to him, so I've learnt to put up with him."

"I wonder how well he really knows him," she said.

"Oh, pretty well, I think. Peter's quite perceptive."

"Is that what you think?" Her voice was dry. "But I suppose you see a side of him the rest of us don't. He's always seemed to me pretty blind. Or perverse. I'm not sure which it is. He actually likes that man, does he?"

I looked at her uneasily. "Beryl, did he say something specially offensive to you while Henrietta and I were upstairs? He stopped as soon as we came in. But was it something even worse than the kind of thing he said after that?"

"Wasn't that bad enough?" Beryl asked. "It took me by surprise, of course, that he should think I was the right person to tell how much he'd enjoyed the fire. I think he's horrible. But he and Peter are really close friends, are they?"

"I'm not sure about that exactly," I said. "I think he's just a sort of habit of Peter's. One of the crosses he feels he has to bear because Simon somehow seems genuinely attached to him. Peter isn't hard enough to shake off someone who cares for him, and on the whole, I'm glad he isn't."

"I see. Well, good night, Freda. I'm very tired. And thanks for everything."

She went on upstairs and I went into the living-room, where I found Peter and Simon seated on either side of the fire, looking as if neither of them was even aware of the presence of the other. That, I thought, was one of the advantages of a really old friendship. You could afford to ignore one another. When you were very tired, as I could see that Peter was, you need make no effort to please.

I went to him and put a hand on his shoulder.

"Since Simon's got to sleep down here," I said, "I think we might leave him to it. Let's go to bed."

"Don't worry about me," Simon said quickly. "I shan't go to sleep for hours. My whole nervous system feels so stimulated, I expect I'll stay awake till dawn."

Peter got to his feet. "Still, I think Freda and I will leave you to it. Good night."

"Good night," Simon answered, and returned to his contemplation of the dying fire.

Upstairs Peter apparently did not want to talk and when I told him that before he returned to the cottage Simon had behaved really unforgiveably to Henrietta and Beryl, he only looked abstracted, as if he wished I would be quiet. I knew the withdrawn look on his face and accepted the fact that this was one of the times when it was best to leave him alone. I myself would have liked to talk for a little while, in a quiet way, to calm down after the fever of the evening, for like Simon, I felt overstimulated and wide awake, although I was tired. In bed I could not even keep my eyes shut, but lay staring upwards in the darkness.

I was not sure how much time had passed when I heard Peter say softly, "Freda?"

He had been lying completely still and I had not been sure if he had been asleep or awake.

"Yes?" I said.

"Mind if we talk a little?"

"Go on."

"What would you say if I'd done something stupid—

really damned stupid—and something that can't be un-done?"

It was not in the least what I had expected. With a doubtful laugh I said, "How can I possibly tell if I don't know what it is?"

"But just in a general way . . . No, I see you can't say anything."

"Why not tell me what it is? Possibly it isn't really stupid at all."

"Oh, it is—though it mightn't have been if things had turned out differently."

I felt a curious little stab of fear. "Peter, it isn't something to do with the fire, is it?"

"Do you mean, did I set fire to the house? No, I'm not as far gone as that."

"Well, what is it?" But he did not answer and after a moment I went on, "Beryl thinks the fire was started by a short in the roof. Apparently there was a tangle of old wiring up there which she thought was dangerous, but Henrietta wouldn't have the place rewired because of the expense."

"The fire didn't start in the roof."

I was startled. "How d'you know?"

"I talked to some of the firemen. They think it started in the garage and that sparks from it fell on the thatch and set it alight. If it had spread on the ground level first, I don't suppose Henrietta would have had a hope in hell of getting out alive, and perhaps not Beryl either."

"But what would start a fire in the garage?"

The garage had once been a carriage-house and was at one end of the old building, at the opposite end to the kitchen, where Beryl had said she had been. That must have been how the fire had been able to take a hold on the house without her becoming aware of it. Like the rest of the house, the garage had been roofed with thatch.

"Perhaps something to do with the wiring there," Peter

replied. "It had a light in it and the wires were probably as old as everywhere else. I don't suppose they'll ever know exactly what happened."

"Is anything left of the house?"

"A little, but not enough to make it worth anyone's while to try to rebuild it. It'll have to be demolished."

"What will happen then?"

"I imagine Henrietta will sell the site. She may get quite a good price for it."

"But who's going to buy it? What's going to be built there?"

"Your guess is as good as mine."

"I wonder if it will affect us in any way. I mean, if it's something hideous, or even a factory or something. They've been talking, haven't they, of developing the Alcaster district?"

Again he did not answer for a little while, then he slid an arm under my head and said very quietly, "Freda, are you happy here?"

Once more he had taken me by surprise. "Why d'you ask that?"

"I was only thinking of what Martin said at lunch. He said all the Cosgroves exploit their women. Am I exploiting you, living as we do?"

"It's my impression that it was mostly my idea that we should live like this," I said. "What I've not been certain of lately is how well it was suiting you."

"Well, I'm not sure of that myself. I sometimes have a feeling that a change would help. But I'm not sure that isn't a kind of chronic instability that I ought to try and conquer, or life may be hell for you."

"I think you're taking Martin too seriously. He was just making conversation. But you were wrong about him, you know. He isn't mean. He was the one who suggested we should all contribute to help Henrietta."

"Yes, perhaps I've never been fair to him, or else real success has mellowed him."

"If you want us to move away, Peter, I'll move."

"Well, this isn't a good time to think seriously about things like that, is it? We can talk about it later, if we want to, when we're on our own. Now let's see if we can get some sleep."

He kissed me gently and withdrew his arm. A few minutes later I could tell by his breathing that he was asleep, though I remained wakeful for some time longer.

I was wondering how it would feel to leave this uncomfortable little cottage where I had spent most of my life and to think of strangers moving into it, perhaps strangers with lots of money who would build on to it and completely alter its character, so that with the old house up the lane burnt down there would be nothing for nostalgia to feed on and draw me back to Ickfield. Presently I fell asleep without having remembered that when Peter had started to talk to me in the darkness of our bedroom he had asked me how I would feel if he had done something stupid. Something very stupid. Something, he had said, that could not be undone, which for some reason had made it sound sinister. But he had not got around to telling me what it was.

In the morning I still did not remember it, for while I was busy getting breakfast for our enlarged household, arranging a tray to take up to Henrietta so that she could have breakfast in bed, my thoughts were suddenly distracted by a ring at the front doorbell and when I went to answer it, I found two strange men on the doorstep who introduced themselves as Detective Superintendent Beddowes and Sergeant Mason.

CHAPTER 4

Superintendent Beddowes said he had heard that the elder Mrs. Cosgrove was staying with us and that he would be glad of a chance to talk to her.

I said, "She's still in bed and I'd hate to disturb her. She's eighty and she's got a bad heart and she had a very rough time yesterday."

The superintendent said that of course he understood. "But perhaps we could speak to you and your husband now and see the other lady later."

"Yes. Come in." With a horrible sense of foreboding that I knew exactly why the men had come, I let them into the living-room and closed the door behind them. "I'm making coffee," I said. "May I give you some?"

"Now that would be really nice," the superintendent said, "if it isn't any trouble."

He was a burly man with a square, strong face, blunt features, grizzled hair and small grey eyes that seemed to be constantly on the move, never lingering on anything for more than a moment. The sergeant was a much younger man, taller and slimmer, with a healthy pink face, smooth black hair, which he wore rather long, and a silky black moustache.

"If you'll sit down," I said, "I'll bring it in in a minute and I'll fetch my husband."

But first, I thought, I would finish preparing Henrietta's tray and take it up to her. I had no intention of mentioning that there were police downstairs, but Henrietta, who was sitting up in bed when I went into her room, had heard men's voices downstairs and asked who they were.

"Two policemen," I answered, "and they'd like to talk to you presently, but I shouldn't get up before you're ready."

I thought she looked very old and frail this morning and I wondered if she had slept at all. But her eyes, considering me thoughtfully, were alert.

"Police," she murmured. "D'you know, I've been half-expecting them. Well, I'll be down soon."

I left her and went to the bathroom, where Peter was shaving.

"There are two policemen downstairs," I said. "They want to talk to us. Come down as soon as you can."

As I was speaking Beryl came out of the room where she had slept. She was wearing the dress that had been ruined the evening before.

"Police?" she said. "About the fire?"

"Of course," I said.

"But does that mean . . . ?" She stopped, letting her mouth stay a little open. Her face had gone white.

"Possibly," I said, since the meaning of the unfinished sentence was obvious. "But perhaps they'd have come in any case. I suppose there always have to be inquiries after a fire. I expect they'd like to talk to you too."

I went downstairs again, followed by Beryl, who went straight to the living-room, while I returned to the kitchen to finish making the coffee. I could hear her introducing herself to the two detectives. She sounded calm and controlled, as if she had got over the first shock of hearing they were there. A minute or two later, by the time I had a tray ready with coffee for everyone, Peter had come down and joined the group in the living-room.

As the superintendent took the cup I handed to him, he said that this was fine and just what you wanted on a cold morning when you had been up since God knew when. His roving glance rested briefly on my face, then dwelt for a little longer on Beryl's, and then dived into his coffee cup, where it stayed for a little while.

"I believe, Miss Cosgrove, you were in the house when the fire started," he said.

"I was," Beryl replied.

"Your brother—" He snatched a brief glance at Peter. "You are brother and sister, I believe."

"We are," Peter answered.

"And the elder Mrs. Cosgrove is your mother?"

"Our stepmother."

"Ah yes. I just like to get things clear. What I was about to say was that one of the firemen had a talk with Mr. Cosgrove yesterday evening and mentioned the fact to me that Mrs. Cosgrove and yourself, Miss Cosgrove, had been in the house when the fire started."

"That's correct," Beryl said.

"Where were you?"

"In the kitchen," she said. "We'd had a birthday party for my stepmother, who's just eighty, and there was still some clearing up to be done."

"Can you tell me how you first became aware that the house was on fire?"

Beryl frowned, sipping her coffee. "D'you know, I can't really remember? It's a thing I've been asking myself. If I'd noticed it sooner, perhaps I could have done something."

"I very much doubt that," he said. "If a fire once starts in one of those old buildings, it goes up like a torch. It's almost a miracle Mrs. Cosgrove got out alive and you yourself were lucky enough, by the sound of things. But can't you remember anything about the beginning of it?"

"Well, of course, a little. I smelt burning, but for a few minutes I thought it was just someone lighting a bonfire somewhere, though it was rather late in the evening for that. I mean, it was quite dark. But it just didn't occur to me it was in the house itself. And then suddenly I realized it was and that it couldn't possibly be coming from out of doors—"

She turned her head sharply as the door opened and Simon came quietly in.

After spending the night on the sofa in the living-room, he had got up when I came down to get breakfast, had neatly folded his bedding and taken it upstairs and had got dressed in our bedroom after Peter and I had left it. The excitement that had exalted him the evening before seemed to have burnt itself out and he looked more than usually subdued. When Peter introduced him to the two police-men, Simon merely nodded distantly, accepted a cup of coffee and sat down as unobtrusively as he could in a corner of the room.

Beryl looked at him with sharp dislike and lost the thread of what she had been saying.

Mr. Beddowes prompted her. "You realized the smell of burning couldn't be coming from out of doors."

She took her head in her hands. "Yes, that's where things get sort of confused. I know I rushed out into the hall and there was a kind of wall of smoke in front of me. It seemed to be pouring down the stairs and I could hear crackling. I thought of my stepmother, who I knew was in her room. I think I tried to go up the stairs, but I was blinded by the smoke and I couldn't breathe, so I staggered out of doors instead and ran straight into my brother . . ." She shuddered violently. "It was all so horrible. I felt so helpless. When I saw someone putting a ladder against the house, I couldn't take in at first what was happening. I didn't even recognize Mr. Ormerod. I only began to come to myself when I saw my stepmother climbing out of the window. The relief was so wonderful."

Mr. Beddowes nodded. "Yes, indeed, I can understand that. But now that you've had a little time to think over what happened, have you any theories as to how the fire started?"

"I think there must have been a short in the roof," she answered. "There's a sort of attic up there—or there was— and there was some old wiring trailing over the rafters. The house badly needed rewiring, but my stepmother was worried about the expense of it."

"It was your impression that the fire started in the roof?" he said.

"Didn't it?" she asked.

"According to the evidence we have at present," he said, "it started in the garage, which was probably set alight deliberately. There's a can in the wreckage there that had certainly contained petrol, and if that had been set alight, it would have been as effective as a petrol bomb. And everyone knows how to make those nowadays. You can get it from television."

She stared at him blankly, then exclaimed, "Arson!"

I was hardly surprised. This was what I had been expecting ever since the detectives had arrived. And even before that, after my talk with Peter in the night, when he had told me that the fire had started in the garage, a premonition of something more to come, something that I shrank from even thinking about, had lingered at the back of my mind. I looked at Peter to see if he seemed to share my feeling, but I could tell nothing from the expression on his face.

He said, "There've been several cases of arson in the neighbourhood recently, haven't there?"

"Yes," the superintendent answered. "It looks as if there's a maniac loose. But there's been nothing so far on the scale of the fire last night. It's been a case of garden sheds and one derelict house, due to be demolished anyway, and an office building that was always empty at night. In fact, nothing that endangered life and limb."

"I suppose the fellow's taste for destruction has been growing," Peter said. "The thought of a little murder thrown in could have added to the zest of the thing."

"Could be," Mr. Beddowes agreed. "Or it could be that last night we had someone else at work. And as I must allow for that possibility, I should like to begin my inquiries with a few questions which you can answer or not, as you choose, but if you will, I'll be grateful."

"Where we all were?" Peter said. "What we were doing between the time we came back from my stepmother's party and the outbreak of the fire?"

"Exactly," the superintendent said. "If you'd begin, Mr. Cosgrove."

"Well, I think it was about four o'clock when my wife and I got back from the party," Peter said. "Wasn't it, Freda?"

"Just about," I said.

"And I went upstairs to do a little work," he went on. "I'm a writer of sorts and I work in a room upstairs. I didn't get much done, but I stayed there till my wife called out to me that the other house was on fire. I'm afraid it isn't much of an alibi, though I suppose if I'd left the house during that time my wife would have heard me."

"Thank you. And you, Mrs. Cosgrove?" Mr. Beddowes looked at me.

I might have said that I had fallen asleep in my chair by the fire and so would not have known if Peter had left the house or not, but I did not feel compelled to mention this.

"I just stayed in here, doing nothing in particular, until I smelt the smoke," I said. "I've no alibi either."

"But I don't think either of us has a motive," Peter said. "Don't you want to know about our motives, as much as our movements?"

"I'll come to that in a moment," Mr. Beddowes said gravely. "Mr. Edge, d'you mind telling us how you spent the evening?"

Simon started. He seemed to have withdrawn into a dream from which he returned only with some reluctance. He stared hard at the superintendent, apparently trying to concentrate, until Mr. Beddowes repeated what he had just said.

"Oh," Simon said. "Oh yes. Yes, I see. Of course." He stuck there.

"You were at Mrs. Cosgrove's birthday party, were you?" Mr. Beddowes asked patiently.

"No, of course not," Simon answered. "It was a strictly family affair. I'd never even met Mrs. Cosgrove. Peter and Freda are old friends of mine, and I'd dropped in on them a few days ago and they very kindly asked me to stay on, but I've never met any of the rest of the family."

"Then how did you spend the afternoon and the evening?"

"Well, let me see." Simon put the tips of his fingers together and his small monkey-face crinkled in what appeared to be a great effort to remember, as if he had been asked what he had been doing a month ago, and not merely yesterday. "When Peter and Freda set out I cooked myself an omelet," he said, "and made some coffee and started reading the newspaper—but you aren't interested in anything as early as that, are you?"

"Never mind, go on."

"Well, then I had a bit of a nap and after that I made myself some tea."

"And then?"

"Then Peter and Freda came back and we talked for a little while and then I went for a walk."

"What time would that be?"

"I haven't the faintest idea. I haven't any sense of time. I don't even wear a watch. I had one once—it was given to me by a dear old aunt of mine—but I pawned it and never bothered to redeem it, even when I could have. Got on just as well without it. What's a watch but a reminder of death, ticking away the minutes of one's life? Not that I'm afraid of the idea of death—no more, I mean, than everyone is—

but I don't like the idea of *measuring* the time I've got left."

"Quite," Mr. Beddowes said. "But if you were still in the house when Mr. and Mrs. Cosgrove returned from the party, we may take it you set out for your walk sometime after four o'clock."

Simon thought it over carefully, then nodded. "Yes."

"Wasn't it getting rather dark for a walk by then?"

Simon's face brightened. "Yes—oh yes, it was. But that's when I like going for a walk. You meet no one. You're all alone in a world of infinite promise. D'you understand that? Darkness is so immeasurably rich. There are no limits to it. It could contain anything and everything. My greatest joy is to go walking in the dark."

"I see. Well, where did you go?"

"I'm afraid I don't know," Simon answered.

"Oh come, you know perfectly well," Peter said irritably. "You've prowled around this neighbourhood often enough. You probably know it better than I do."

"But I don't know the names of places," Simon said. "I couldn't say I crossed this field or that—they've all got names, haven't they?—or went past this farm or that farm, or anything of that sort. I could *take* you where I went, Superintendent, if you'd like me to do that."

Mr. Beddowes did not look at all attracted by the idea of going on a long and almost certainly unfruitful ramble through the cold December countryside.

"Did you go anywhere near Mrs. Cosgrove's house?" he asked.

"Oh yes!" Simon cried excitedly. "That's where I ended up. I was coming back down the lane from the crossroads when I saw the glow in the sky ahead of me, so of course I sprinted on to see what was happening. And believe me, I've never been so thrilled in my life as I was when I saw it —the fire, I mean, and the people watching, the red light

on their faces and the red light you could see in their souls
as they gloried in it, fear and lust just blazing in them,
quite as exciting as the fire itself—"

"Stop him, stop him!" Beryl suddenly shrieked, clapping
her hands over her ears. "I can't bear it when he talks like
that!"

He gave her a puzzled look, as if her feelings were quite
beyond his comprehension.

Peter glowered at him, saying, "Yes, you needn't plug
that line any more. We've all had enough of it." Then he
turned back to Mr. Beddowes. "You said you'd come back
to the question of motive. Are you going to tell us anything
about that?"

The superintendent and the sergeant exchanged glances.
Mr. Beddowes seemed to hesitate for a moment, then he
said, "It's something that may have nothing to do with the
fire. It's just something very strange. You know the house
wasn't totally destroyed. Some of it at the back is still
standing, though it's pretty well gutted. But the firemen got
it under control at last. The bathroom and the bedroom
next to it are only half burnt out. And the cupboard between them is a black ruin, but you can still see some of
what was in it. And what was in it was a skeleton. Charred
and black, like everything else, but there's no question at
all about what it was. A woman's skeleton."

A slight cry came from the doorway. Henrietta was
standing there and had heard what the superintendent had
just said.

"But there isn't any cupboard between the bathroom and
the bedroom," she said. "There never has been."

She advanced into the room. She was wearing the
sweater and skirt that she had borrowed from me the evening before and her red velvet slippers. Her face was bewildered rather than horrified. She seemed to be assuming
that Mr. Beddowes was talking nonsense.

Beryl backed her up. "No, there's never been a cupboard there."

I was ready to say the same. I had known the old house well and remembered clearly that between the door of the bathroom and that of the bedroom next to it there had only been a plain wall, covered with wallpaper of grey and white stripes, like the other walls of the passage.

But Mr. Beddowes shook his head. "There's a cupboard there. It looks as if it may have been a child's toy-cupboard. We found a few things in it, some toy soldiers and a toy pistol, that weren't destroyed in the blaze. And the skeleton."

Henrietta sat down, her head trembling slightly in a way that made her look really old.

"I've lived in that house for twenty years," she said, "and there's never been a cupboard there. I suppose the fact is, at some time it must have been papered over. You must talk to Mrs. Kenworthy about it. She and her brothers decorated the house for my husband and me while we were abroad, and I'm sure they'll tell you it never occurred to them there was any cupboard between the bathroom and the bedroom. How long ago do you think the skeleton was put into the cupboard?"

"We can't tell yet," Mr. Beddowes answered. "There's nothing left but a skull and charred bones. I don't know if the forensic people will be able to tell us anything. They haven't had time yet to come up with an answer."

"All the same," Peter said, trying to catch and hold the superintendent's evasive glance, "this isn't only a case of arson, is it? It's murder. That's why someone as senior as a superintendent has appeared here."

There was silence in the room. It was only brief, yet it gave me a sense of its stretching out indefinitely with increasingly painful tension. When Mr. Beddowes spoke, his voice sounded almost reassuring.

"We can't be certain of that, Mr. Cosgrove," he said. "For all we know, the skeleton was just something that belonged to a medical student, say, an anatomical specimen that he threw into the cupboard when he'd no further use for it."

"And then concealed the cupboard by papering it over?" Peter said. "Does that seem likely?"

"Well yes, there's that." Mr. Beddowes stroked his square jaw. "Yes, there's that."

*

"I don't think old Mr. and Mrs. Ormerod can have known anything about it," Henrietta said. "They're the people from whom my husband bought the house."

"I was going to ask about that," Mr. Beddowes said. "They'd a son, hadn't they?"

"Yes, Max Ormerod, who saved me from the fire last night," she answered. "He's curator of the Alcaster Museum. Why?"

"I thought it would be interesting to find out if he remembers a cupboard between the bathroom and the bedroom," Mr. Beddowes explained, "or was it already concealed when his family moved into the house?"

"I suppose it might have been done years before," she said. "Even centuries. One can't possibly guess what tragedies and crimes old houses like that may have covered up."

"Except that the toy soldiers we found are in the uniform of the First World War," Mr. Beddowes said, "and the pistol's a toy of about that time too."

Henrietta frowned, trying to work it out, then she turned to me.

"Freda, you've lived here longer than any of us. Do you know when the Ormerods took the house?"

"They were always there, as far back as I can remember," I said. "I've a feeling I was told they bought the house when Max was born, but I can't be sure of it."

"And he's about thirty-five, isn't he?" she said. "So he wouldn't have been there to play with toy soldiers during the First World War. Do you know anything about the people who lived there before the Ormerods?"

I shook my head. "Only that their name was Smith, but I don't think they lived here long, and I don't know who lived in the house before them."

"And you can't remember ever hearing talk of anyone disappearing mysteriously, or perhaps just going away to Australia, or something like that, in connection with these Smiths or Mr. and Mrs. Ormerod?" Mr. Beddowes asked.

I again shook my head. "But I was only ten, you know, when Professor and Mrs. Cosgrove moved in. If I'd heard of anyone going away, I shouldn't have paid much attention. Grown-up people were always coming and going."

"And all these years I've lived with a skeleton in that cupboard!" Henrietta cried, plainly meaning it to be taken literally and not as an ill-timed joke. "I do remember thinking once that the bathroom wall was extremely thick, but so were a lot of the other walls in the house, so I didn't give it any thought. I hope you don't find any more cupboards with old bones in them, Superintendent. I hope I haven't been living in a morgue."

He stood up. "If there were any others, the fire's finished them off, but I think one's enough to be going on with. Thank you for all your help. You've told me the main thing I came here to ask—was there, to your knowledge, a cupboard between the bathroom and the bedroom? And you've been very definite that there wasn't." He signalled to the sergeant, who also rose. "We'll look in on Mrs. Kenworthy and on Mr. Ormerod too. We'll see what he has to tell us. I suppose at this time of day he'll be at the museum. Good day."

Peter opened the door for them and the two men went out to their waiting car.

As soon as they had gone Beryl sprang up and went to the telephone.

"I'm going to tell Max about this," she said. "I'd like to know what he's got to say about it. And I ought to tell him that I shan't be in to work today, though I shouldn't think he expects it. And I'll tell Grace the police are coming and ask her if she noticed anything peculiar between the bathroom and the bedroom when she and the others decorated the house. They'd never have thought of papering over a perfectly useful cupboard themselves for no particular reason, would they?"

"Anyway, not without looking inside," Peter said, "and if they'd stumbled on a skeleton, I don't suppose they'd have kept it to themselves."

Beryl dialled the number of the museum. While she was talking to Max and afterwards to Grace, I went out to the kitchen, made more coffee and some toast and set them out on the dining-table in the living-room. I could not stop myself thinking about my childish memory of Martin, standing on a step-ladder, swathed in a roll of wallpaper which had slid out of his grasp and wrapped itself around him. He had been laughing cheerfully at his own clumsiness, a young man who even the ten-year-old child that I had been had thought was astonishingly handsome and carefree and charming.

Which room had that been in? I thought it must have been the one that was to become the drawing-room. Certainly it had not been in the passage upstairs, and certainly, laughing so light-heartedly, he could have had no suspicion of the gruesome secret hidden up there.

I wondered how Max Ormerod had answered Beryl on the telephone. Had he any memory from his childhood of a cupboard being papered over? It seemed extremely unlikely. The toys that had been found in it were too old for them to have been his, and besides, it felt impossible to imagine the old Ormerods, so generous with their Mars Bars and toffee, not only committing murder, but then cold-bloodedly concealing the corpse in their own house and going on contentedly living with it there for a number of years. I began to think about the Smiths, trying to remember anything that I had heard about them, but they were merely shadowy figures to me, so vague that I did not even know how many of them there had been. Had there been just a couple, or had there been a family? And how long had they lived there? They had come and gone, leaving no trace behind them.

When Beryl had finished her telephoning, she said nothing about what Max or Grace had said to her, except that Grace would be coming to the cottage shortly and that probably, in view of the fact that the fire had been arson and the discovery of the mysterious skeleton, her brothers and Vanessa would not leave that day in case the police should want to question them. All the same, Grace had said, she would make them move out to The Green Man and so make room for Henrietta and Beryl in her house, since there really could not be room for them to stay in the cottage. Yet Beryl looked curiously disturbed. I thought that something that either Max or Grace had said must have upset her unexpectedly and brought a very troubled frown to her face. She was silent throughout breakfast and afterwards went upstairs, saying that she would tidy up the rooms that she and Henrietta had used.

Grace, Martin, Luke and Vanessa arrived together about eleven o'clock. Grace said that the superintendent and the sergeant had been to see them and she was volubly indignant because she and her brothers had been asked to account for their movements between the end of Henrietta's birthday party and the outbreak of the fire.

"As if we needed alibis!" she exclaimed. "In fact, we spent the evening playing bridge, but he looked as if he found that highly suspicious. Isn't it absurd? It's obvious the thing was done by the maniac who's been setting things on fire in the neighbourhood for the last few months. If the fire had started inside the house, it might have been different, but anyone could have got into the garage from outside. It was never locked. They ought to be hunting for him instead of bothering us."

"I'd be surprised if they really suspect any of us," Martin said. "What motive could any of us have for burning the house down? None of us benefits, and none of us has such a hatred of Henrietta that we'd want to destroy her home just for the hell of it. None of us, to the best of my knowledge, is a lunatic. But they've got us all gathered together here at the moment, so it's natural for them to question us while they've the chance. I thought it quite sensible of them. I didn't resent it."

"I'm glad you said to the best of your knowledge none of us is a lunatic," Vanessa said. "It's a well-known fact that lunatics often deceive their nearest and dearest about their sanity more easily than anyone else. Look at the men who murder woman after woman while living perfectly happily with an unsuspecting wife."

"I see," Martin said, with a chilling smile. "And which of us do you in your wisdom suspect of being an arsonist?"

"But that's the point, don't you see?" She said. "One doesn't suspect them."

"I expect I'm high on her list," Luke said in his mild, ironic voice. "It's true I was playing bridge with the rest of you when the fire broke out, but I'm an ingenious chap. I could easily have left a time bomb in the garage, set to go off when I'd an alibi. Besides, being what most people take for a fairly inoffensive character, it probably seems only too likely that under the surface I'm seething with aggression."

As he spoke it struck me suddenly that they were all talking about the fire, but not one of them had mentioned the skeleton. It seemed strange, when I came to think of it, that it did not seem to interest them. It was almost as if, by common consent, they were avoiding the subject. But that was not a comfortable thought, although, once it had occurred to me, I found it difficult to get it out of my head.

It was Simon who succeeded in making me forget it. He was sitting again where he had sat before in a corner of the room, as if he wanted to be as unobtrusive as possible. Giving a gentle little cough, he said, "I can suggest several motives for burning the house down."

All the Cosgroves turned to look at him, and as they did so I was struck, as I often had been before, by how like they were to one another and also how united they were. Even Peter and Beryl, though they lacked the strong, rather hard features of the older family, were obviously Cosgroves.

Martin raised his heavy eyebrows haughtily. "Who's this?" he asked, as if he really had not noticed Simon's presence in the room until then, and as if, now that he had done so, he thought Simon had no right to be there.

Peter introduced him. Simon stood up and sauntered to the middle of the room.

"It's important to remember," he said, sounding like a lecturer starting to address a class, "that the fire and the skeleton may have nothing to do with one another. But let's begin by supposing they have and supposing the incendiary knew the skeleton was there. He might have burnt the house down for two quite different reasons. One could have been that he wanted to destroy the skeleton, and so, one must assume, destroy the only remaining evidence of a crime he'd committed long ago, but which he'd always had a ghastly fear might somehow come to light. And it was just his bad luck that the part of the house where the old cupboard was, was the one part that wasn't totally destroyed. If it had been, and then just a few old bones had been found in the wreckage later, I don't suppose anyone would ever have been able to explain how they'd got there, and he would have been quite safe."

All the Cosgrove faces looked struck with astonishment. It was as if they could not bring themselves to believe that they were being addressed in words the implications of which were so insulting.

Simon, enjoying the attention of his audience, however hostile it was, went on almost casually, "The other reason is virtually the opposite of that one. It still means someone must have known the skeleton was there, but in this case what he wanted was to have the old crime brought to light. He probably didn't realize how the fire would rage through the house, once it got a grip, and hoped the cupboard would be exposed without being destroyed. It was just his good luck that it wasn't destroyed and the skeleton was preserved. And if this explanation happens to be the right one, I imagine we can assume his motive was revenge. Something, after twenty years or more, made him want the murderer to be exposed. Perhaps he'd been brooding on it all this time till he became a bit unbalanced, and he had the bright idea that if he set fire to the house the crime could be discovered without anyone finding out that he'd known about it himself and stayed quiet. The fact that Mrs. and Miss Cosgrove might have been killed didn't matter to him. Probably, with what must have become a sort of monomania by now, he never gave it a thought. As I said, I think this fellow I'm talking about is distinctly unbalanced."

He paused, giving Martin time to say icily, "Have you any more to say?"

"Good Lord, yes," Simon answered. "I've only been talking about the possibilities that the arson and the skeleton are linked together. But suppose they aren't. Suppose the corpse went into the cupboard with the toy soldiers and the pistol around sixty years ago. The chances are then that the murderer himself is safely dead by now, beyond the reach of human justice. Don't you like that phrase, beyond the reach of human justice? It took me by surprise when I came out with it. It implies all kinds of things I never think about at all. I'm not sure, you know, if there's such a thing as justice, human or otherwise—"

"For God's sake, say what you've got to say, or shut your bloody mouth!" Martin snarled. "Get the farce over, then we'll take Henrietta and Beryl back to Grace's house. I don't actually know why we're listening to you."

"Because you're so interested, of course," Simon replied. "You aren't sure if I'm merely outrageous, or if I'm going to say something strikingly intelligent. Well, suppose that old crime had nothing to do with the fire, then what stares you in the face about it? It's that there were some quite valuable pictures in the house and if someone happened to covet them, what simpler way could there be of disguising the fact that he'd stolen them than burned the house down? You none of you know for sure, do you, whether or not those pictures went up in the flames? You've probably been assuming they did, but suppose they didn't."

"So now we're thieves, as well as arsonists and murderers," Grace said. "Peter, if I may say so, you have the most peculiar friends."

"Thieves *or* murderers," Simon corrected her. "Haven't I made it clear it's unlikely that anyone could have been both?"

"All the same, you're trying to make out, whatever happened, it was done by one of us!" Grace said. "One of the people in this room!"

"Oh, not necessarily," Simon said. "Anyone could have got into the garage to light the fire, and all kinds of people must have known Mrs. Cosgrove had the Bullers and thought they were worth making off with."

"If I may offer an opinion," Vanessa said in her crispest voice, which demanded a hearing, "I don't think we should forget Mr. Everett Baynes. He knew Henrietta had the pictures. He knew their value. He coveted them. He seems to me an obvious suspect."

"For heaven's sake, I spoke to him at Claridge's," I said. "He's got a perfect alibi."

"How do you know it was Mr. Baynes you spoke to?" Vanessa asked. "Whoever it was, I presume he had an American accent, but he could have been an accomplice, couldn't he, standing in for Mr. Baynes while he was here? Or perhaps it was Mr. Baynes you spoke to and the theft was carried out by someone in his pay. What do you know about him, Henrietta? He may be a gangster or something."

Luke gave an apologetic little laugh. "I'm afraid Vanessa's been making a too profound study of Peter's books. She's learnt the art of picking on the unlikeliest character as the criminal."

"I wonder which of us is the likeliest," Henrietta said.

"Oh, I am, I am!" Simon cried. "Isn't that obvious? Isn't that why I've been doing my best to lead you all astray with my nonsense? I knew about the pictures and their value. I know some crooked art dealers who'd give me a good price for them. That price might not be significant for the rest of you, but it would be for me. I'm always hard up. And I've a habit of going out for long walks in the darkness. I knew everyone would be tired after the party and it would be easy to get into the house. And I was there on the scene very soon after the fire got started, and I made no secret of how much I enjoyed it because I knew I couldn't conceal how exultant I felt at the success of my plans. Of course it was a shock when I realized Mrs. Cosgrove was trapped upstairs, but if someone hadn't turned up to rescue her, I'd have done it myself. My God, if I was one of you, I'd have me arrested on the spot."

"Exhibitionist," Martin said contemptuously. "Henrietta, shall we be going? My car's outside."

Henrietta got to her feet. "Very well. Freda and Peter,

my dears, thank you both so much for looking after me last night." She kissed us both. "Now if I could borrow some sort of overcoat, Freda, as I'm sure it's cold outside. And Mr. Edge, if you've got the pictures, I hope you make a nice profit out of them. For myself, I must trust to the insurance. Grace, will you be able to take Beryl and me shopping this afternoon? We really must get some clothes, and I must return what I've got on to Freda."

Chatting to Grace about a shopping expedition to Alcaster while I went to fetch a sheepskin jacket for her, Henrietta went to the door, then led the way out to Martin's car.

Beryl was the last to leave the cottage. She lingered behind the others for a moment to say in my ear, "Freda, that man's horrible. He's evil. If I were you, I'd make Peter turn him out. There's a devil in him. He's dangerous."

CHAPTER 5

Simon gave no further signs of being dangerous after the Cosgroves had gone. Annexing the newspaper, he settled down behind it and said no more for some time. Peter went upstairs to work and I went to the kitchen, meaning when I had stacked the dishwasher with the breakfast things, to make some pheasant pâté for a party in the evening of the next day for which I had been asked to do the catering. I had cooked the pheasant a few days before and left it in the freezer and should have taken it out to thaw not later than yesterday. Not surprisingly, however, I had forgotten to do this and now found the bird rock-hard. Making the pâté would be impossible.

I tried to think of something else I might do in preparation for the party, but found that my mind was so disorganized that I could not concentrate. If I went ahead with anything, I thought, I was certain to make some hopeless blunder. Returning to the living-room, I found that Peter had also given up the attempt to work, had managed to rescue the newspaper from Simon and was sitting by the fire, doing the crossword, while Simon was sitting on the hearthrug and gazing dreamily into the flames.

As I came in, he looked up and said, "This man Baynes who that woman thinks may have stolen the Bullers—who is he?"

Peter filled in a word in the crossword before he answered. "She didn't really think so," he said. "It was just her way of attracting attention to herself. In a room with Martin in it she's always scared she may not be noticed."

"But I think it was an interesting idea," Simon said. "Who is the man?"

Peter told him what Henrietta had said about Everett Baynes.

"I see, I see," Simon said. "And he was expected today to give an opinion on the Bullers. That's suggestive, isn't it?"

Peter was scribbling absently. "Of what?" he asked.

"Well, I've always had my doubts about them," Simon said. "There are a lot of fakes of his stuff about, you know. That's always liable to happen when an artist comes rather suddenly into fashion. No one really knows anything much about him yet, they just buy him up because they've been told it'll be a good investment, and even the dealers haven't made enough of a study of him to be reliable. I believe you told me once Mrs. Cosgrove got the pictures from Max Ormerod."

"That's right," Peter said.

"I wonder how much he knows about Buller."

Peter looked up from his crossword and gave Simon a long, curious stare. "Just what are you getting at, Simon?"

"Nothing—oh, nothing really," Simon answered blandly.

But Peter's interest was aroused. "You said there was something suggestive about the fact that an expert was expected today to give an opinion on the Bullers. You actually think the house might have been burnt down to prevent that happening?"

"That isn't impossible, is it?"

"So Max is our arsonist, that's what you want us to think. He knew he'd sold Henrietta fakes and burnt the house down so that she shouldn't find him out."

"You don't think much of the idea?"

Peter's expression was oddly amused. "It strikes me as utter nonsense," he said.

"But I don't see why he shouldn't be the arsonist," Simon went on. "The fact that he rescued the old woman after the fire got going doesn't mean he didn't start it. He probably hadn't realized she was upstairs and was going to be trapped, and though he may have wanted the pictures destroyed, he needn't have meant to commit murder. It accounts for his being on the spot, doesn't it?"

"But we don't even know if he knew Baynes was expected."

"Your sister could have told him. She works with him, doesn't she?"

"I'm not sure she knew about Baynes herself."

Simon smiled suddenly. "Well, if you don't like my theory, I'll admit I don't think so very much of it myself. I was just trying it out on you."

"I'd stop worrying about it, if I were you," Peter said. "We know we've a pyromaniac in the neighbourhood. I'd say the fire was obviously his work. In any case, it's a job for the police."

He returned to his crossword. But Simon would not leave him in peace. Picking up the poker, he gave the fire an unnecessary jab. He was frowning heavily.

"All the same, I wish I knew what happened to the Bullers," he said. "Were they burnt or stolen?"

"Does it matter so very much?" I asked. "In either case, Henrietta will get the insurance."

"Is that what they mean to you—money?" Simon demanded. "They're works of art, you know."

"I thought you thought they were fakes."

"Some fakes are as good as the genuine thing," he said earnestly. He returned to contemplation of the fire.

He remained quiet after that and gave the impression of being oddly depressed, as if the almost certain destruction of the Bullers really meant more to him than I would have expected. But then I noticed that as he drank a pint of beer and ate his sandwich lunch he seemed to grow increasingly tense. For once he seemed to have time on his mind; I saw him glancing at the clock on the mantelpiece more than once, which was unusual in him, because, as he had told Mr. Beddowes, he was normally genuinely indifferent to time. Though he was reasonably punctual for meals, this always had the appearance of being accidental. He was waiting for something, expecting something, I thought, though what it could be in his singularly aimless life I could not imagine until, about half past two, the telephone rang.

He sprang to his feet, then slowly sat down again, apparently remembering that as a guest here, it was not for him to answer it. But he kept his gaze anxiously fixed on it while Peter picked it up, spoke into it, listened, then turned to Simon.

"It's for you," he said.

A broad smile lit up Simon's face. He took the the telephone and said, "Simon Edge here."

Someone spoke to him and he said, "Yes . . . Yes, certainly . . . Most satisfactory . . . Excellent . . . Yes, that will suit me very well . . . Thank you. Goodbye."

Putting the telephone down, he stood still for a moment, gazing straight before him, then he exultantly rubbed his hands together.

"Good news?" I asked.

"Yes, something I've been waiting for ever since I got here and worrying about a good deal when it didn't come. If it hadn't come this afternoon, I'd have given up hope." He turned to me, slid an arm round my waist and kissed me on the tip of my ear. "Darling Freda, you'll soon be rid of me. That ought to cheer you up."

He did not often indulge in endearments and I could have done without this one, but the thought that he might be going to leave the cottage made me feel better disposed towards him than usual.

"Have you sold a picture or something?" I asked.

"Yes," he said, "a lovely picture. Such a nice one. I ought to have got more than they're offering, but one mustn't expect the moon." He chuckled. "You've hated having me here, haven't you, you poor dear? You try to hide your feelings to please Peter, but I can tell. I can always tell. And the sad thing is, I think of you two as my best friends. But one doesn't honestly like many of one's friends, does one? Peter doesn't really like me any better than you do, yet he'd be sad if I disappeared out of his life. He'd probably come looking for me to see what he'd done to offend me. Friendship isn't a case of liking at all, it's mostly habit."

"Oh, shut up," Peter said, looking irritated and not at all interested in analyzing his feelings for Simon. "I'm glad you've sold a picture, but you're staying here for Christmas, aren't you?"

I thought it had not been necessary for him to say that, but luckily Simon answered, "Well, I'm not sure about that now. I think I'll probably be off."

"Who is she?" Peter asked.

"Who is who?"

"The woman who bought the picture."

"Oh, you mean the one who telephoned. She isn't actually buying the picture herself, she just made the contact. Very nice of her too." Simon gave another gleeful little chuckle. "Am I the person who sometimes speaks contemptuously of money? I'll tell you my real feelings about it. It's the best stuff in the world. And I'll tell you what, I'll take you both out to dinner this evening. If you'll lend me a little, I can definitely pay you back in a few days. Is there a nice pub in the neighbourhood where one can get really good food, not just bar snacks, but an honest-to-goodness meal? What about that place, The Green Man? Wouldn't you like that?"

"Thanks for the thought, but perhaps another time," Peter said. "I don't think Freda or I are feeling much like celebrating."

"Of course you're not—stupid of me. I'm feeling so cheerful myself, I simply forgot your calamity for the moment. I suppose it really is a calamity for everyone concerned. One can't help wondering . . . Still, I shouldn't say that. If it's all right with you now, I think I'll lie down for a bit before I go for my walk. I didn't actually get much sleep last night, though the sofa was perfectly comfortable. It was just that I was too excited. And naturally I'm excited now. I suppose if one were a great success and money kept rolling in day after day, one would get used to it and stop caring about it, but I can't help thinking about it nearly all the time, either with hatred when I haven't got any, or with exquisite love when I have. The perfect example of a love-hate relationship."

"Oh, go to bed," Peter said. "You talk too much."

"I do, I do, it's true. Well, I'll see you presently." Simon bounced out of the room, and Peter and I could hear him as he went leaping up the stairs to the bedroom that was his again.

Peter stretched out his legs, crossed his ankles, folded his hands on his stomach and closed his eyes. I tried doing the same. I would have been glad to sleep for a little, but the attempt to do so only had the result of making me restless, and after a few minutes I sat up, smoothed my hair back from my face, rubbed my eyes and said, "Is he right that you don't like him, Peter?"

Peter did not open his eyes immediately and I began to think he had really fallen asleep and that I ought not to disturb him. But then, opening them, he answered, "I don't know. Probably. I don't think I like many people much. They interest me, I like to have them around so that I can watch them and think about them, but as for *liking* them . . . I love a few, but that's much easier."

I nodded. "That's what I'd have expected of you. You're too tolerant to be capable of much real liking. But I believe that little horror likes both of us very much and I honestly can't bear him. I've a strong feeling about him, so in my way I'm more like him than you are."

"Oh, now you're getting too complicated for me," Peter said. "What's for supper?"

"I haven't thought about it yet. Perhaps I'll make a stew of some sort."

"Good, I like that."

"How much d'you think he got for his picture?"

"Not very much. If it was only twenty pounds, he'd get excited."

"D'you think he'd really have taken us out to dinner if you hadn't turned him down?"

"It seemed to me best not to put him to the test. Anyway, he needs the money too much to throw it around on that sort of thing." Peter closed his eyes again. But then he opened them, though he did not look at me, but at some vague spot beyond me where he seemed to see something that puzzled him. "Freda . . ."

"Yes?"

"That woman who rang up . . ."

"What about her?"

"Oh, nothing. Something odd, but it's probably nothing." Again he closed his eyes and this time they stayed closed and I felt sure after a minute or two that he had fallen asleep.

It was some time later, as the dusk was deepening outside the windows and I had switched on the light in the room and drawn the curtains that Simon came downstairs and set out for his usual walk. By then I had made a stew and left it simmering on the stove and Peter had woken up and gone up to his workroom. The typewriter thudded spasmodically. I telephoned Grace to ask how Henrietta was and was told that she was resting, but that, considering what she had been through, she seemed surprisingly well. Grace had taken her and Beryl into Alcaster to buy some

clothes and they had had visits during the day from an insurance assessor and a young man from the local newspaper who appeared to have been told nothing by the police
about the skeleton in the cupboard and to be interested
only in the fire.

"So of course we said nothing about the skeleton," Grace
said, "and I suggest you don't either if he gets around to
you, or we'll have the national press down on us."

I agreed and had only just put the telephone down when
the doorbell rang. I thought it might be the young man
from the Alcaster *Chronicle* and went to open the door,
but it was Max Ormerod who stood there. He looked cold
and white, standing in the patch of light that fell on him
from the doorway. He gave his little twitching smile.

"I just dropped in to ask how things are," he said. "I
won't stay if you're busy."

"Oh, come in, Max," I said. "I'm glad someone's come."

"But if you're busy . . ." He remained diffidently on the
doorstep.

"I'm not," I said. "I can't settle to anything. Come in
and have a drink."

"But Peter's busy." He had heard the typewriter.

"He won't mind stopping." I closed the door behind Max
as he came into the room and adjusted the velvet curtain
over it. Going to the bottom of the stairs, I called up to
Peter, "Max is here."

Max took off the quilted anorak he was wearing and
dropped it on a chair.

"I haven't been able to settle to anything either today,"
he said. "There was a rather important meeting in the afternoon and I couldn't concentrate. I don't know why.
Mrs. Cosgrove and Beryl are safe and that old house didn't
mean anything special to me, even though it was my home
when I was a child. I remember I hated leaving it, but
that's so long ago, I quite stopped caring. Yet I've been on
edge all day."

"The after-effects of heroism," I suggested. "What you did was really very heroic, you know. That wall might have come crashing down on you at any minute. What will you have—whisky?"

"Thank you." He held out his thin hands to the fire. "The police came to see me this morning. I expect they've been to see you."

Peter came into the room as he was speaking. He took over the drinks and poured out whisky for all three of us.

"Did they want to know about the cupboard?" he asked. "The one that's appeared mysteriously between the bathroom and the bedroom."

"Yes. It's very peculiar, isn't it?" Max took a glass from Peter and sat down on the sofa where Simon had spent the night.

"Then you don't remember any cupboard there?" Peter said as he also sat down.

"Well, I do—I think I do," Max answered. "I think it was my toy-cupboard. That bedroom was my playroom and I had bookshelves in it and a table and a chair or two and a toy railway that sprawled all over the floor, but most of my toys were kept in a cupboard in the passage."

"That's extraordinary," Peter said. "You're sure we're talking about the same cupboard? There wasn't another?"

"Not to my knowledge. I suppose it isn't impossible that there could have been, if it had been papered over." Max frowned in thought. "Now that you mention it, I can't absolutely swear there wasn't another cupboard because my memory of the place isn't as clear as it might be, and though I often visited Mrs. Cosgrove, I'd no reason to go upstairs."

"What about the fact that the toys they found in the cupboard, the soldiers and the pistol, were too old for them to have been yours?"

"But they *were* mine," Max replied. "They were given to me by my father. They'd been his when he was a child. The soldiers were in the uniform of the fourteen-eighteen war, and I think the pistol belonged to the same period. It just fired off caps, and I used to love jumping out on people and firing it in their faces and shouting, 'You're dead!' I was a rather blood-thirsty child."

"Most children are," Peter said. "But you're really sure of that, are you? I mean, that the toys were yours."

"Oh yes, absolutely sure."

"Then that proves we're talking about the same cupboard. There wasn't another one."

"But that means . . ." I began, but broke off as Peter frowned at me.

"D'you remember anything about the sale of the house?" he asked. "I mean, did your parents put it in the hands of an agent or sell it direct to my father? I was at Oxford at the time. I don't know much about it."

"Of course you're worrying about how the skeleton could have got there," Max said. "It's very puzzling. Yes, I think we put the house in the hands of an agent and a good many people came round before your father bought it."

"Did you always show them round yourselves, or did you ever just give the keys to the agent and leave it to him?"

Max shook his head helplessly. "It's so hard to remember after all this time. You mean, did we move out before we sold the house so that the agents could have thought that an empty house like that was a useful sort of place to dump a corpse? The agents, I'm fairly sure, were Hepburn and Hepburn. They were a husband and wife, very solid, respectable sort of people. I think he was on the Council. And they're both dead now, so it's too late to question them."

"What I was wondering," Peter said, "is whether they might have handed over the keys to someone who perhaps kept them over a week-end, or anyway for several days, so that he'd time to hide a body there and do a job of repapering."

Horrified, I broke in, "But there'd have been a *smell*, Peter—an awful one! You can't just leave a body to rot in a cupboard without anyone noticing it."

"You might, if you took care to seal it up very carefully."

"But the new wallpaper wouldn't have matched the rest of the passage."

I saw that I was annoying him, that he wanted me to support the theory that he was developing, and I thought that I knew why, but I found it very difficult to be silent. However, I accepted the fact that it would be better to argue with him about it after Max had left.

"As a matter of fact," Max said, "the wallpaper might not have been noticed because the walls were just white, and if one patch happened to look a little newer than the rest it might not have caught the agent's eye. It's an interesting idea, Peter. Have you suggested it to the police?"

"I've only just thought of it," Peter answered. "Until you said you thought you remembered the cupboard I'd been assuming it was papered over before your parents bought the house. As for the smell, even if it did get out, it may only have put off a few possible purchasers, who thought it was the drains and didn't make an offer when otherwise they might have done. Of course, by the time my father and Henrietta moved in after their trip round the world, it would have gone."

Max nodded thoughtfully. "Yes, now you mention it, I think if I'd a dead body to dispose of, someone else's empty house would be a quite good place to leave it. I wonder if Hepburn and Hepburn kept a record of the people who looked round the houses they were looking after. I shouldn't think they did. Anyway, the people who took the firm over several years ago wouldn't have kept them. I don't suppose there's any chance of tracing all the people who had the keys. And to go by what the police told me about the state of the skeleton after the fire, I don't suppose they'll ever identify her. How does Mrs. Cosgrove feel about it? Does it worry her very much to discover she's been sharing her house with a corpse?"

"It's hard to tell with her," Peter said. "She's very tough. She doesn't give her feelings away."

"But she's quite well after her ordeal?"

"So far as we know."

"That's good, that's good. For a moment, when she collapsed at the foot of the ladder, you know, I thought she might be finished, but she pulled round wonderfully." Max finished his whisky and stood up. "That's what I came round to ask. I've always admired her."

"Don't go yet," Peter said. "There's something I'd like to ask you now you're here. It's about the Bullers. Simon's been saying they might be fakes. Is there any possibility, d'you think, that he's right?"

Max sat down again. He began to smile, a small smile at first, then it broadened, then he burst out laughing.

"What a man!" he said. "He really said that?"

"He said he thinks it's probable, though he admits he's never seen them."

"Well, that's a lie."

"That he's never seen them?"

"Of course. I found them through him. Didn't he tell you that?"

*

Peter shook his head. "I don't think I've ever heard just how you found them. It was in some antique shop, wasn't it?"

"Yes, it was Edge who put me on to them. D'you remember, I'd met him here when he was on a visit to you, and then I ran into him by chance one day when I was in London and he told me how he'd come across two paintings which he was prepared to swear were Francis Bullers in an antique shop in Brighton, and he thought I might be

specially interested in them because he was certain one of
them was of Mrs. Cosgrove's house and the other of the
church in Ickfield. He said he'd have bought them himself
if he'd been able to afford them, but cheap though they
were he hadn't got the money. Anyway, he got me interested and Brighton wasn't far, so I decided to go and take
a look at them and there was no doubt about it, they were
paintings of my old home and the church here. So I bought
them. I'm not sure if it was because I was hoping they'd
turn out an investment, or if I meant to keep them, but you
know what happened. I showed them to Mrs. Cosgrove, as
I was sure she'd be interested in them, and she fell in love
with them. She didn't actually ask me for them, but I saw
she wanted them, so I offered them to her for what I'd paid
for them. If they were fakes . . ." Max started to laugh
again. "D'you realize it was probably Edge himself who
painted them and planted them for me to find? I imagine
the dealer was in on it with him and got a cut of the price."

I remembered how Simon had said very earnestly that
fakes were sometimes as good as the genuine thing. It was
possible that he was very proud of his work.

"But suppose he hadn't met you that day in London," I
said. "You said it was by chance. What would he have
done with them then?"

"Oh, he'd probably have made contact with me some
other way. Or he might have gone straight to Mrs. Cosgrove. Anyway, what does it matter, now that the pictures
have gone up in smoke?" He stood up again. "I'll be going
now. It's been a rather upsetting day, with the police coming and all that. By the way, I told them I couldn't be sure
about the cupboard. Well, good night. My best wishes to
Mrs. Cosgrove."

He picked up his anorak and slipped it on and Peter let
him out of the door.

The moment he had closed it again, I broke out, "Peter,
what on earth did you mean by all that talk about house

agents and about someone they gave the keys to leaving a body there? You know it's nonsense and you know what the truth is you've got to face, don't you?"

He returned to the fire and sat down beside it. He did not look at me and did not answer until I repeated my question. Then he gave a long sigh, looked up at me and met my eyes.

"Let's not make up our minds what the truth is till we know a lot more than we do," he said.

"But, Peter, if the toy-cupboard was there when the Ormerods lived in the house," I said, "and I think Max is only being vague about it because he thinks it may help us, isn't it certain it must have been Martin, or Luke, or Grace, or the whole lot of them together, who covered it up? They'd already taken it into their heads to decorate the house, so it would have been very easy for them."

"Which makes one or all of them murderers, doesn't it?"

"Well?"

"You really think that?"

"I think it's got to be considered."

"You take it remarkably coolly."

"Not really." I went over to him, sat down on the arm of his chair and put an arm round his shoulders. But he stayed rigid and after a moment I got up, went out to the kitchen and gave a stir to the stew. Returning to the living-room, I said, "I know it's different for me, I'm not one of the family, but I believe that sooner or later you're going to have to face the fact that they sealed up that cupboard, and it may be best for you to face it straight away."

"And the corpse, who was she?" Peter asked.

"I can only suggest one possibility, but of course there may be others."

"Louise?"

"So you're worrying about that already, are you?" I said. "That's why you concocted your theory about the house agents and their clients."

"It's a perfectly tenable theory."

"It's nonsense. I shouldn't try it on the police. It'll only make them wonder what you're trying to hide."

"Louise married an airline pilot and went away to America," he said stubbornly.

"And has never been heard of since, has she?"

"I don't know. It isn't the kind of thing I'd think of asking Martin."

"But she was here when they were decorating the house. I remember her clearly. I remember how beautiful she was. And then, as I remember the way the story goes, she left him only a few days after they got back to London. And an airline pilot, who may be almost anywhere in the world at any time, is a very convenient sort of husband for someone to be supposed to have when in reality she's just disappeared."

"You seem to have it all thought out."

"I've been thinking about it ever since that detective told us about the skeleton in the cupboard this morning. And so have you, haven't you?"

He gave another sigh. "All right, I have."

"What are you going to do about it?"

"Nothing."

"Nothing at all?"

"Nothing at all. Martin's my brother. He can be a bastard, but he isn't a murderer."

"I wish I felt as sure of it as you. I can't help thinking that one of the reasons why he wouldn't come to visit Henrietta if he could help it was that he hated and feared the house because of what had happened there. I used to think it was snobbery—because he's become so successful he'd no time for us—but yesterday I didn't think that fitted him at all."

Peter was silent again, watching me in a curiously wary way.

"What are *you* going to do about it?" he asked at last.

"Nothing, of course, if you aren't," I answered.

"You mean that?"

"For God's sake, Peter, we've been married two years—haven't you learnt to trust me yet? What did you think I was going to do? Go to the police and pour all this out?"

He seemed to consider this carefully, then he gave a slight, rueful smile. "I'm sorry. I'm a fool, aren't I? I do trust you, you know—completely. I knew you didn't mean to go to the police. But the thing's a nightmare and a characteristic of nightmares is that one loses one's way in them. And you're right that it's best for us to face the thing, because the police are going to get on to it without any help from us, and we ought to have thought out what line we mean to take when that happens. I can't decide whether or not we ought to warn Martin. He'll only deny everything, but it might make him take his position seriously." He gave a short laugh. "D'you remember how quickly he came up with the suggestion that we should all help Henrietta financially when Vanessa started trying to persuade her to sell the house. And Grace and Luke couldn't wait to support him. It puzzled me, because, as I've told you, Martin's mean. But Vanessa, of course, wasn't here when the trouble must have happened, whatever it was. She wasn't married to Luke yet. She didn't realize what a threat it would have been to Martin and the others if Henrietta had thought of moving."

"But the house was destroyed that very evening and the skeleton was found," I said. "I can't make anything of that. No one gained by the fire."

"You know, I think we'll have to settle for our pyromaniac," Peter said. "That makes better sense than anything else I can think of."

I nodded. "And since I've seen the way Simon enjoyed the fire, I can understand a bit better than I did how the lust for fire gets hold of a person. Talking of Simon, he's taking a pretty long walk this evening. The stew'll be ready by now. I suppose we've got to wait for him."

"Give him a little longer, anyway. Let's have another drink."

He got up and poured out drinks and we settled down to wait for Simon.

But in the end we got tired of waiting and I laid the table and dished up the stew. We had finished the meal and cleared up, leaving some stew to keep warm for Simon, before we heard the squeak of the garden gate, which I assumed meant that he had returned from his walk. Then there were footsteps on the path, but they were too firm and heavy for his and a moment later the doorbell rang. Simon would not have rung, he would have come straight in.

Peter went to the door and opened it.

Sergeant Mason stood there. Light rain was falling and there was moisture on his pink cheeks that looked almost like tears and there was a dewy sheen on his silky black moustache. He stood there, looking embarrassed, and when Peter invited him in, did not move.

"I'm very sorry, sir," he said, "I'm afraid I've some bad news for you. I believe Mr. Edge is a friend of yours."

I had come to Peter's side as he stood in the doorway.

"Yes," he said. "What's wrong?"

"He's met with an accident," the sergeant answered. "He seems to have been hit by a car. A car that didn't stop. Out beyond that Roman villa near the crossroads. He was found by another motorist who was on his way to The Green Man."

"Is he hurt badly?" Peter asked quickly.

"He's dead, sir. I came to ask you, as you're his friend and I believe he was staying with you, if you'd be so good as to come to the hospital to identify him."

CHAPTER 6

While Peter was gone a mood of guilt took hold of me. It was guilt because I had not liked Simon better, and it would never have occurred if I had not been told that he was dead. I knew that being dead does not improve a person's character or make them any more likeable than they were when they were alive, but to speak ill of the dead is a very profound taboo. I had lost people whom I loved and knew what grief was, but I had never before lost anyone whom I had actively disliked, and my feelings about it were disturbing and confused.

I tried to remember everything good about Simon that I could. There was his continuing affection for Peter, which I was sure had been genuine. There was his weird form of sincerity, which was one of the things that made him intolerable, but which was simply the result of the fact that he could not hide his feelings. However disgraceful they were, he betrayed them. There was his relatively good-humoured acceptance of poverty and failure.

Was there anything else?

It seemed a small crop of virtues for a human being to have accumulated in forty years of life, and it might be my fault rather than his that I could not think of any others, but I really could not. Given a little time, I knew, I would not even try to do so. Once the awesome fact of death had receded into the past, I would remember him merely as that dreadful little man whom I did not miss in the least. For the moment, however, the thought of him lying on a mortuary slab, probably stiffening and cold already, made me feel a chill in my own blood that made me shiver internally although the room was warm.

Peter returned about an hour later with Superintendent Beddowes and Sergeant Mason. Except for a brief greeting from Mr. Beddowes, they did not speak to me, but went straight upstairs to the little room that had been occupied by Simon, where, after a few minutes, Peter left the two of them and came down to join me in the living-room.

"What is it?" I asked him, feeling that I must speak in a whisper, although the two detectives upstairs could not possibly hear what I said.

"I'll tell you presently," Peter whispered back and turned away from me, standing as close as he could to the fire, as if he felt the same chill as I did.

We could hear the men upstairs moving about and talking occasionally, then after a little while coming down the stairs. When they came into the living-room the sergeant was carrying Simon's rucksack, stuffed full with what looked like all that he had brought with him to the cottage.

"And you've his address in London?" Mr. Beddowes said to Peter.

Peter went to the bureau in a corner of the room, found an address book in it and read out Simon's Islington address. Mr. Beddowes wrote it down, said good evening to me and he and the sergeant left.

As soon as they had gone Peter poured out a whisky for himself, then suddenly remembered that I might like one too and looked at me with raised eyebrows. I nodded and he poured out a second drink.

Taking mine, I said, "Well?"

"It's murder," he answered.

I had guessed by then that that was what he would say, but I could not restrain a shudder.

"What happened?"

He sat down on one side of the fire and I sat down facing him.

"He was hit on the head with something heavy," he said, "then dumped in the road and deliberately run over by a car. If the car had gone over his head, they probably couldn't have been sure it wasn't an accident, but it went over his chest instead. It was a badly botched job. Then it happens that because of the rain earlier, they could see his footsteps as far as that small car park in front of the dig. He must have stood there, waiting for someone, because they could see his footsteps by the edge of the road, rather deeper than the ones leading up to the place. But the rain had stopped, you see, by the time he was killed, so they hadn't been washed away."

"In front of the dig," I said. "Why there, I wonder?"

"Just an easy place to describe, if you wanted to arrange a meeting. And there's very little traffic along there in the evening."

"But how was it arranged . . . ? Oh!" I exclaimed. "The telephone call he had in the afternoon."

Peter nodded. "Of course."

"So it wasn't anything to do with the sale of a picture."

"No, but I think it was something to do with money. He was expecting to be paid some pretty sizeable sum and he couldn't conceal his delight. He never could."

"I suppose it wasn't for the Bullers. If he'd taken them before the fire and had a customer—"

"No," Peter said positively, "it had nothing to do with the Bullers. D'you know what I think?"

"Go ahead."

"I think he saw who started the fire yesterday. While he was walking past the house in the dark he couldn't be seen himself, but he could have seen something suspicious happening at the garage and stood and watched. And in the crowd of people who turned up later he could have spoken to someone and murmured that he wanted money. Blackmail. I wouldn't put it past him."

I looked at him wonderingly. His thin cheeks looked

more hollow than usual and his very bright blue eyes, which could look so youthful and innocent, looked bitter and hurt.

"You *did* care for him, didn't you?" I said quietly. "Whatever you said."

"I suppose so," he admitted reluctantly. "Yes, I did. We'd known each other for such years, and when we first met I thought I'd never met anyone so amusing and vital. It took me some time to begin to find him out and by then I was used to him, I almost needed him. It can be an important thing, you know, if you've enough memories in common. You share something that seems to matter. But— well, I knew he was a crook. I mean, I knew, for instance, that he faked paintings and did it extremely cleverly. I went to his studio a few times and saw some of the things he'd done. But I never thought he'd sink to blackmail. And yet, now I know he almost certainly did, it somehow doesn't surprise me."

"That telephone call you answered," I said, "you said there was something odd about it. What was it?"

Again Peter seemed reluctant to answer. "She didn't say much," he said at length. "Just, 'May I speak to Mr. Edge, please?' But it sounded—only I can't be sure—I thought it sounded foreign."

"Foreign!" I exclaimed. "You don't mean . . . Oh, it can't be!"

"Ilse Klein? No, as you say, it can't be."

But we met one another's eyes with a kind of shrinking look, as if the thought that we had both had were somehow unspeakable.

Ilse Klein was a woman in her seventies who had lived in Ickfield since the nineteen thirties. She had come as a refugee from Germany, taking work as a housekeeper with a family who had lived in what was then the manor house and now was an old people's home. In Berlin she had been a teacher of music and gradually, along with the domestic work that she had done, she had managed to build up a small connection in Alcaster, teaching the piano. After a little while she had been able to give up the domestic work and rely on her teaching. But as she had grown older her hands had become very arthritic and she had had to give up the teaching too. She now lived on her old-age pension in a very small cottage, rented to her by her first employer, and was a solitary, bitter woman who rebuffed nearly all attempts at friendship, sure that in these there was only patronage or pity.

She had accepted Peter, with his gift of penetrating the defences of the most dissimilar people, more than she had most people, and he had a certain affection for the proud old woman, though she had almost none for the country that had sheltered her, and no regard for the neighbours who would have been kind enough to her if she had allowed it. Peter always maintained that she would have turned out just the same if she had never been driven from her home because she was one of the people born with a grudge against life, and that if she had been able to remain in Berlin and perhaps become a successful teacher of music there, she would still have found reasons for turning her back on the world. Solitary as she was, she had never learnt good English and still spoke with a strong foreign accent.

"No, it couldn't have been Ilse," I said. "You couldn't blackmail her for what you called a sizeable sum. She's got no money to pay with."

"No," Peter agreed.

All the same, as we continued to look at one another, deep uneasiness came into the eyes of both of us.

After a moment Peter went on, "But it's possible Simon might not have demanded much from her. Didn't he say he ought to have got more than he was being offered, but one mustn't expect the moon? I think he was the sort of person who just might squeeze ten or twenty pounds out of a victim for the sense of power it gave him."

"You realize that what you're saying is that Ilse may be our arsonist?" I said. "She may be the person who's been lighting fires around the place. Is she really as crazy as that?"

"I don't know. She just might be. I believe arsonists are sometimes old, lonely, cranky, but absolutely respectable people who get some peculiar bee in their bonnets. But I don't know why she should hit on Henrietta's house. I don't think she's any special grudge against Henrietta."

"And even if she could have lit fires, surely she couldn't have managed to murder Simon in the way you told me. She does drive around the country is that awful little rattletrap car of hers and she could have run him down, but I can't see her being able to knock him down with a blow on the head and drag him into the road so that she could run over him."

"No, that's quite true. We're talking nonsense, aren't we?"

"But you're sure whoever telephoned had a foreign accent?"

"Yes. But it would have been easy to assume, I suppose."

"But you're sure it was a woman's voice?"

"Yes. Yes, I think so. The fact is . . ." He paused. He looked as if he meant to go on, but then he was silent. There was something about that telephone call that he was keeping to himself.

"Peter, have you some idea you recognized the voice?" I asked.

"No," he said quickly. Perhaps too quickly.

"What did you tell the police about it?"

"Only what she said and that it sounded foreign."

"You did say that—that it sounded foreign?"

"Yes."

"Then they're going to suspect Ilse, aren't they?"

He stirred uncomfortably. "Perhaps. I rather wish I hadn't said anything about it. But I don't suppose they'll bother her too much. They can't suspect her of the murder, any more than we do."

"Then aren't we back to thinking it was someone in the family?"

For a moment Peter looked at me almost as though he hated me, but he brushed a hand across his face, blotting out the expression. He stood up.

"I don't see why," he said. "Just tell me a good motive any of us has for burning the house down. Now I'm going to bed. If it weren't so late, I'd go round to see Grace. I don't know if she and the others have heard about Simon yet. But they're probably all in bed by now. We can go in the morning."

He put the fire-screen in front of the remains of the fire and went upstairs.

As I followed him I thought that next day I must get to work on the preparations for the party for which I was doing the catering. I wished that there were some way that I could get out of it, but I was enough of a professional to feel that, short of genuine illness, I had an obligation to stick to my commitments. Arson and murder did not provide an adequate excuse for breaking a promise. So Peter would have to go by himself to Grace's house, or so I thought until the next morning, when I woke up much earlier than usual and found myself so restless that I got up without waking Peter, put on my dressing-gown and went down to the kitchen and made the pheasant pâté and the filling for a quantity of little lobster patties before it was time to make coffee for breakfast.

Peter and I had had it and got dressed by about half past nine when we set out together to visit Grace.

The morning was damp and still with a sky of heavy

cloud, which threatened rain later. When we reached the ruins of Henrietta's house, we found that a notice had been fixed to the gate. "Danger. Keep Out." Nevertheless, two boys of about ten years old were scrambling about among the blackened beams and fallen walls, occasionally throwing charred objects that they had found at one another and looking for treasure. Peter went in and chased them out. When they were at a safe distance from him, they turned and made faces at him and gave mocking, ear-splitting whistles before they made off.

Returning to me, he said, "Silly little bastards, don't they realize I only did it for their own safety and not just to spoil their fun? What's left could come crashing down at any time."

As Superintendent Beddowes had told us, it was the back of the house that still stood. It was of brick, not lath and plaster, and although, like the rest of the house, it was very old, it must have been built at a somewhat later date. There was an unpleasant smell of sodden ashes in the air which was indescribably mournful. The windows in the few bits of wall that had not crumbled had lost their glass and looked vacantly blind. There was a sense of death about it. Yet we lingered, looking at it, strangely fascinated.

"I hope they get on soon with clearing it all away," I said. "It's horrible now."

"But what will they put up instead?"

"Does it matter to us, if we aren't staying?"

"Aren't we staying?"

"I don't know. At the moment I wish we were far away. Don't you get a feeling of doom in the air? I keep saying to myself, 'What next?' "

"As a matter of fact, so do I, though it isn't rational."

"Except that the solution of what's happened may be as horrifying as the things themselves. You're afraid of that, aren't you?"

He did not answer.

After a little I went on, "You're afraid of something, Peter. I know that telephone call upset you."

Instead of answering me, he asked me a question. "How important is loyalty, Freda?"

I gave him a quick look and saw that he was still gazing at the black ruin before us.

"Are you thinking of loyalty to Simon and whether or not he was worth it?" I asked.

"I was just thinking about it in a general way," he said. "Loyalty to something good isn't any problem, is it, if one's got the courage for it? But is there any virtue, can one take any credit to oneself, for loyalty to something rotten?"

"Probably not," I said.

"That's really what you think?" He looked put out, as if it had not been the answer he wanted.

"Well, think of all the loyalty that's gone in recent times to causes that go in simply for bestial crimes," I said. "I can't see any virtue of any kind in that."

"Then you see it almost as a kind of vice. It shouldn't be indulged in too freely."

"Well, isn't it like that sometimes? Like courage. Very evil people sometimes have lots of courage, and it would be better for everyone if they had a bit less."

"In fact, loyalty and courage only become virtues in the right context. By themselves it seems you don't think they mean much."

"But, Peter, your loyalty to Simon hasn't done any harm to anyone," I said. "Not even to him because it really wasn't your fault that letting him stay here ended in his getting murdered. Blackmailers always run that risk, wherever they are, I should say. You shouldn't worry about it."

"I'm sure you're right." He smiled, though I had the impression that he had paid no attention to what I had just said. But he put an arm round me and gave me a sudden kiss on the temple. "Now let's get on. I wonder if Grace and the others know about Simon yet."

We knew the answer to that before we reached Grace's house, for as we were walking along the road that bordered the village green we saw the police car with Superintendent Beddowes and Sergeant Mason in it drive away from Grace's gate. We also saw Martin's Bentley in the road in front of the pleasant, sprawling Georgian house where she lived, so we knew that the rest of the family had already assembled there.

It was Beryl who answered the door to us when we knocked. Her round, plump face was pale with anger and her hazel eyes, behind her large round glasses, looked more staringly prominent than usual.

"Didn't I tell you that man was dangerous?" she said furiously to Peter. "Didn't I say he was frightful?"

He and I were taking off the anoraks we were both wearing.

"He certainly seems to have been dangerous to himself," he said, "but what have you to complain about?"

"Don't you realize those two men have just been here, asking us all for our alibis?" She was almost shrieking. "Our *alibis!* As if one of us could be a murderer!"

*

Through the open door of the drawing-room behind her Martin spoke authoritatively. "For God's sake, don't make such a fuss! They're only doing their jobs, and you've nothing to worry about—you and Henrietta. Nor have Luke and Vanessa, if an alibi from a husband or wife is worth anything. Grace and I are the ones who find it hardest to account for ourselves. So stop that caterwauling and start doing a little thinking, like a reasonable person."

Beryl swung round and went into the drawing-room. She was wearing a very new-looking, light green woollen blouse and skirt, the result, no doubt, of her shopping trip into Alcaster the afternoon before. Peter and I followed her into the room.

"Peter and I have no alibis, except what we can give one another," I said. "We spent the evening at home, waiting for Simon to come in for supper, but I don't get the feeling either of us is suspected of murder. It takes more than the lack of an alibi to make one a good suspect."

In the big, pleasant room, furnished without much regard for taste, but only for comfort, Grace was standing with her back to one of the windows, looking solidly planted there, as if she expected to have to resist some form of attack. Martin, even more formidably, had taken possession of the hearthrug. Luke and Vanessa were sitting side by side on the sofa, and Henrietta was sitting very upright on a stiff little Victorian chair, looking paler than usual and with her lips pressed tightly together, as if she were holding in something that she wanted to say. She was wearing a straight grey jersey dress and low-heeled black slippers, the result, like the clothes that Beryl was wearing, of yesterday's shopping expedition.

She spoke quietly as Peter and I came in. "Peter, no one's said yet how sorry we all are about your friend. I know you were very attached to him."

He stooped over to kiss her. "You may be sorry, Henrietta, but I don't think anyone else is, unless it's for themselves. And perhaps with reason. Freda and I have been talking the thing over and we've come to the conclusion Simon was probably killed because he saw who started the fire and was trying a little blackmail. So if you can come up with someone who had a motive for burning the house down, you've got your murderer, haven't you?"

"You're implying that was someone in this room," Martin said with dangerous softness.

"Oh, not necessarily," Peter said. "Simon led a complicated life, and we don't know what he saw."

"I think you're quite wrong," Beryl said. She was moving restlessly about the room, unable to make up her mind whether or not to sit down, and if so, where, like a dog that goes round and round before it can make up its mind where to curl up. "I don't think his murder had anything to do with the fire. I think the fire was the work of that maniac we know we've got in the district, and I think the murder was done by someone who chased him down here from London or somewhere, from whom he'd been hiding. I think that's what he was doing down here, staying with you—he was hiding from someone he was afraid of. People like him must have plenty of enemies."

"You may be right," Peter agreed equably. It worried me, because I did not think that he meant it. "He usually came to stay with us when he was running out of money, but perhaps he'd another reason for it this time. Anyway, you've nothing to worry about if you were with Henrietta round about the time he was killed."

"She was," Henrietta said. "Grace took us into Alcaster to buy some clothes—Freda, I must give you back what you lent me—and when we got home Grace made us some tea, then we settled down to watch television. It was only one of those silly comedy programmes one gets so bored with, but we were both too tired to do anything else."

"Then wasn't Grace with you too?" Peter asked. "Martin said you hadn't an alibi, Grace."

"No, I haven't," she answered. "When Henrietta and Beryl started watching television I took the car and drove to The Green Man. That's highly suspicious, isn't it? I drove right past the spot where I understand they found your friend's body. And I'm pretty strong for a woman, so I think I could have done the job. But the reason I went out was that I wanted to talk to Martin about—about something, but I was told he'd gone out. So I talked to Luke and Vanessa, who were in their room, then I drove home. I think it must have been before the murder, because there weren't any police about, and if Edge was standing by the roadside, waiting for someone, I didn't see him. But I may have missed him by only a few minutes because the rain had stopped by the time I got home, and I gather the police think the murder was done just about then."

"And if you're curious about where I was when Grace came looking for me," Martin said, "though I'm damned if I see why you should take it on yourself to question us, even if Edge was your friend, I'd gone into Alcaster because I wanted to be alone for a bit to do a little thinking. I've got some fairly serious problems on my mind at the moment, things that wouldn't interest you, so I won't go into them, and I haven't had much chance to think about them since I got here. Naturally I expected to be back in London yesterday, but having got stuck here, I decided I'd better give these matters a little attention. So I went into Alcaster and had a drink at the Station Hotel—a horrible place, but it was quiet. I can't tell you the exact time I arrived there, or when I left, but perhaps the waiter will be able to tell you that. He can confirm, anyway, that I was there. Then I drove back to The Green Man and must have missed Grace by only a few minutes because it was still raining when I got in. Like Grace, I didn't see your friend. And like Grace, as the police let me see they realized, I can't prove any of it except that I was in the Station Hotel for a time. And I've done things in my life for which I might conceivably be blackmailed, if I was the kind of person who'd ever pay up. So you never know—perhaps your friend somehow got the information that I was expected in Ickfield and thought he could corner me quietly and put the bite on me, and though I would never pay up, perhaps I wouldn't be above a spot of murder. It's possible, it's possible. I can see a case against myself."

"Don't lay it on too thick, Martin," Luke said in his lazy way. "If you overdo the irony, they'll start suspecting you're trying to cover something up. Speaking for Vanessa and myself, we can confirm you came to our room some time before dinner, but I haven't the least idea what the time was, or if it was still raining or not. We'd been there by ourselves for most of the afternoon. We'd wanted a drink, but we didn't feel like going into the bar and finding ourselves the centre of gossip about the fire, so we had drinks brought up, and the waiter who brought them can say we were both there then, but I could easily have slipped out later and met Edge and killed him. It's true we haven't a car here, as Martin drove us down, but I dare say I could have borrowed one from the garage at the hotel without being noticed and only been gone for a few minutes. You see, we can all make cases against ourselves if we try hard enough."

"But how did any of you know where to find him, tell me that!" Vanessa said sharply, raising her voice as if she were afraid that she might not be heard. "Whoever killed the man knew just where he'd be waiting. Well, how could any of us know that?"

As she spoke, the doorbell rang.

Grace went to the door and the moment she opened it a woman's voice, high-pitched, strident, with a strong foreign accent, exploded over her.

"He is here! That man is here! I go to his house, no one is at home, I come here, I know he is here! Let me speak to him, let me tell him what I think of him!"

"Yes, Miss Klein, of course, but just who is it you want?" Grace said.

"Your brother, your stepbrother, it does not matter what you call him! That Peter Cosgrove who makes as if he is my friend and now says I am a madwoman and a murderess!" Ilse Klein shouted.

Grace brought her into the drawing-room. She came only just through the door, then stood still with her feet apart and her hands clenched at her sides. She was a tall, narrow-shouldered, gaunt woman of about seventy, with scanty grey hair rolled into a small knot at the back of her head, a small, pinched face with burning dark eyes, a thin, high-bridged nose and a small, tight mouth. Probably she had once had a certain beauty and with her delicate features might have had some still if there had been less scorn and bitterness in her face. Just then it looked as if it did not know how to express anything but hatred. She was wearing a stained waterproof, buttoned up to her neck, and Wellington boots.

She ignored everyone in the room but Peter.

"You!" she spat at him. "You tell the police I telephone this man who is killed! You tell them I make an appointment to meet him at the Roman villa. You tell them I burn down Mrs. Cosgrove's house and this man sees me and makes me pay him money. Money—me! I have money to pay anyone! I need all the money I have to stay alive. Do you understand that? Have you ever gone cold or hungry? If he asks me for money, I laugh at him—yes, I laugh! I do not need to murder him, I laugh and laugh!" As she said it, she did indeed begin to laugh, with a dreadful, creaking sound, as if it were something unfamiliar to her, something which she had long ago forgotten how to do.

"But, Ilse, I didn't tell the police you telephoned him," Peter said, while the other Cosgroves stared at the woman in astonishment. "I only told them he had a telephone call in the afternoon from someone who had a foreign accent."

She managed to swallow her laughter.

"And so they come to me—at once they come to me!" she cried. "There are how many people with foreign accents in this country of yours, but they come to me. I have been a British subject for forty years, do you know that, but I am not English. I am British, but I can never be English, that is why they come to me as soon as there is a murder. I burn down houses and I commit murder, all because I am not English. I can live here all my life, I can keep the laws and pay my taxes, but they will never trust me. Never!"

"I'm sure there's some mistake, Miss Klein," Henrietta

said. "Won't you sit down so that we can talk things over
quietly and find out what really happened?"

"And we might have a drink," Martin said. "I could do
with a drink. What about it, Grace?"

"A drink—why should I want a drink?" Ilse Klein re-
torted. "I come to tell you I have a contempt of you. I am
not afraid of you. Tell what lies about me you will, let the
police threaten and abuse me, I am not afraid. I have no
telephone, do you know that? I do not pay for luxuries like
telephones. I have my little car, but that is all, and I do not
use it to run over any man to kill him. I have too much
regard for it, more than I have for any of you. I will go
now."

She turned and strode out of the room, letting herself out
of the front door and slamming it behind her.

"The poor woman," Henrietta said. "I never realized she
was as far gone as that."

"I don't think she is, normally," Peter said. "I think it's
just that a visit from the police is something so terrifying to
her, it's temporarily unbalanced her. She'll calm down
presently. In a good mood she's a rational, interesting
woman."

"But what's all this about a telephone call?" Grace
asked. "The police didn't mention that when they were
here."

Peter told her about the telephone call that Simon had
had in the afternoon before his last fatal evening walk and
about his statement that it concerned the sale of a picture
and his elation after it.

"And it was a woman's voice, was it?" Grace said.
"You're sure of that?"

Peter shrugged his shoulders. "I suppose it just could
have been a man's, disguised, just as the foreign accent
could have been put on, but I think it was a woman's."

"Well, I didn't make it," Vanessa stated flatly.

"Did anybody say you did?" Martin barked at her with the irritation that she always roused in him. "Damn it, why does the woman always try to draw attention to herself? There's no reason to think anyone here made it."

"Only Peter thinks one of us did, can't you see that?" Vanessa said. "You do, don't you, Peter? And that means you think one of us is a murderer."

"Can you *prove* you didn't make the call, Vanessa?" Beryl asked, looking at her with a sudden curiosity that was almost like suspicion.

"Only if you'll accept my word for it," Luke said. "After we had lunch here we went back to The Green Man in Martin's car and we went up to our room then and we were together for the rest of the day and I can guarantee she didn't make any phone call. But of course there's a telephone in our bedroom, so if you think she and I are in this together, no, she can't prove anything."

"Nor can I," Beryl said. "Nor can Grace. Nor can Henrietta. Isn't that funny? So which of us do you think it was, Peter?"

"I thought you all went into Alcaster together, shopping," he answered. "Can't you alibi each other?"

"It depends on when the call was made," she said. "When was it?"

"I think about half past two."

"Then any of us could be guilty. Henrietta was lying down and there's an extension in her room, so she could have made the call without any of us knowing. And Grace and I had washed up the lunch and I was in here, reading the newspaper, waiting till she and Henrietta were ready to go into Alcaster, so I could have made it, because Grace had just gone out to the post office. She said she'd some letters to post, and there's a telephone outside the post office, so she could have made it. We didn't leave for Alcaster till about three o'clock. So take your pick. Which of us do you think it was? That's to say, if you're sure it wasn't the Klein woman, who could have used that public phone box, incidentally, even if she hasn't got a telephone at home."

"There weren't any pips before she spoke," Peter said. "I think the call was made from a private phone."

Something happened in my head just then, a kind of small explosion, which I had felt coming for the last few minutes, but which I had tried to contain, forcing myself to remain silent even when the impulse had come to interrupt, to protest. But now I lost control of it.

"Do you know, there's something extraordinary about all you Cosgroves?" I exclaimed. "You all seem to think that the best way to defend yourselves is to incriminate yourselves. You're all producing all the evidence you can against yourselves. Are you doing it on purpose? Are you all in it together? Have you got some idea that the best way to put the police off the track is to hurl so many suspects at them that they won't know whom to choose? Have you cooked this up because the truth is, one of you is guilty?"

For a moment no one answered, then with one of his most charming smiles, Martin answered, "The clever girl! How she understands us. Only the truth is, you see, Freda, we didn't cook it up. We aren't clever enough for that. It's just the kind of thing we do instinctively. If this turns out to be something in the family, you'll find that's the way we all want to keep it. I think you'll find even Peter wants that —won't you, Peter?"

He and Peter stared at one another, the antagonism that each felt for the other struggling with something else, some deeper feeling that brought out the latent similarity in their faces, which superficially were so different.

"Perhaps," Peter said at length. "But I'm not committing Freda. She isn't a Cosgrove. She may not feel the same as we do."

"Well, Freda?" Martin said, raising his eyebrows questioningly.

"I think, before I promise anything, I want to know a little more than I do," I answered. "For instance, about the skeleton in the cupboard the three of you papered over . . ." I paused there.

"Oh yes, it was Louise," Martin said calmly. "All the same, it wasn't murder."

CHAPTER 7

"It was lunacy," Grace said.

"Utter," Luke agreed.

"But it was your idea," Grace said to him. "You know I was against it."

"Yes—yes, that's true," he said. "It seemed such a simple way of dealing with things when we found the cupboard. But of course it was mad. We were all a little mad in those days."

"It sounds to me as if that may still be the trouble," Peter said. "D'you mind going back to the beginning and telling the rest of us what happened?" He turned back to Martin. "You say it wasn't murder. Can you explain that?"

"Of course. The actual offence of which we're guilty is the concealing of a death," Martin answered. "That isn't nearly as serious as murder and it's done more often than you'd think. Someone dies and the person he's been living with hides the body and goes on drawing his old-age pension, or something of that sort, sometimes for years. It does come out from time to time and you read about it in the papers, but naturally you can be sure there are far more cases of it than ever get discovered."

"So what you're saying is that Louise suddenly died," Peter said, "and for some mysterious reason, instead of behaving normally and calling a doctor, who I suppose would have wanted an inquest since she wasn't a patient of his, and after that having a funeral and having her decently buried or cremated, you bundled her into a cupboard and sealed it up with new wallpaper and left her there for twenty years."

The elder Cosgroves exchanged looks, evidently trying to consult with one another as to the line that it would be best to take.

Then Martin shook his head. "No, it wasn't exactly like that. That was the trouble. I did kill her, you see, but it was an accident. Grace and Luke will corroborate that. They saw it happen. But even with them as witnesses, it might have been hard to convince anyone else because it was common gossip that Louise and I fought like cat and dog. I think the marriage would have broken up pretty soon even if the accident hadn't happened. For one thing, there was someone else I wanted to marry. But of course I couldn't go ahead with that while I was officially waiting for a divorce, and by the time it seemed plausible to say I'd got one the woman in question had gone off and married someone else. And even if she hadn't, I don't think I could have remarried without producing a certificate of some sort to say I was divorced."

"Didn't anyone ever check up on whether or not you really were?" I asked.

"No, they don't, you know," Martin replied. "People usually believe what you tell them about yourself, unless you get too fanciful. I suppose that nowadays someone might take it into his head to investigate what had actually happened, but at that time I was still quite obscure. As a matter of fact, I was just having my first success, and that's partly why we did what we did."

"Please," Henrietta said. She was still sitting very upright on her small chair and spoke crisply, with a sound of authority. "Let's take things in reasonable order. You say you killed Louise by accident, Martin. How did that happen?"

He turned his hands outwards in a gesture of giving in to her and gave a brief sigh.

"We had a stand-up brawl, that's all," he said. "We often did. She'd attack me and I'd hit her back—just a slap on the cheek usually, to stop her going for me with her nails. But that time, unfortunately, we were in the passage upstairs and she stepped backwards and caught her heel in some old carpet we'd taken up but hadn't got rid of yet, and she fell backwards down the stairs and broke her neck. As I say, Grace and Luke saw it happen and they can tell you I hardly touched her."

"If I may say so, you sound somewhat callous," Henrietta said. "Have you no feelings about it?"

"Twenty years is a long time," he answered. "I've had to learn to live with the memory of it. At the time I was shattered. I really don't go in for killing people, you know. It was absolutely the first time I'd done it. I sat and cried real tears for most of the rest of the day, remembering how terribly I'd loved her at the beginning, before I'd found out what a devil's own temper she had. I couldn't bring myself to go near her dead body. It was Grace and Luke who made sure she was dead and who decided what we ought to do—because, you see, it looked fairly probable that I'd be arrested for murder and have to go through the hell of a trial, even if I got a verdict of manslaughter or was acquitted altogether in the end. And there I was, having the first real success of my life. It was that that really turned the scale. It looked as if there was a good chance that my whole career would be ruined."

"I see," Henrietta said. "That would of course weigh with you more than the legal proprieties. Yes, I can see that. But will you tell me why you chose to put her in a cupboard in my house instead of burying her decently in the garden? That would surely have been more reasonable."

"It was the snow," Luke said. "Of course our first thought was to call a doctor. Not Edmund. It wouldn't have been fair on him. But then, when we were absolutely sure Louise was dead, we began to think of all the complications Martin's just told you about. And we were as proud of his success as he was and we wanted to protect it. He'd gone to pieces completely himself. So Grace and I decided the best thing would be to hide Louise's body, and naturally the first thing we thought of was digging a grave in the garden. But there'd been an early fall of snow a few days before and when we went out with spades we found the ground under the snow was rock-hard. So we had to think again and thought of a cupboard, if we could find a suitable one. It would have to be the right kind, which we could conceal, and it was then we realized that the cupboard on the landing would just meet our needs. The doorframe didn't project at all and it was going to be quite easy to paper over it."

A furious exclamation came from Vanessa. "You've never told me a word about all this!"

"Well, no," Luke agreed. "It was much better for your peace of mind to know nothing about it."

"But you ought to have told me!" she cried. "Important things like that—husbands and wives shouldn't keep them from each other."

He looked moved by her concern, but Martin said, "The fact is, we didn't trust you not to bleat it to the first person you happened to meet. I've always thought he'd tell you about it sooner or later and then you'd try to interfere somehow with what, after all, had turned out a perfectly satisfactory arrangement. Henrietta didn't miss her cupboard, which Luke made a very neat job of hiding, and nobody missed Louise. And if it hadn't been for that damned fire the other night, none of this need have come out even now. If you'd been tempted by the idea of selling the house, Henrietta, as Vanessa said you should be, I'd have put in an offer for it immediately, telling you I wanted a house in the country. If I'd done that, I imagine I could have opened up the cupboard and quietly got rid of what was left of poor Louise without anyone noticing. You said you were leaving the house to Beryl, but I didn't think she'd mind having a good lump sum instead. However, the fire put an end to the chance of doing anything like that."

"But since it's resulted in the unfortunate woman's bones coming to light," Henrietta said, still chilly, "may I ask what you intend to do about it?"

Martin looked at Grace, as if he expected an answer to come from her. It reminded me suddenly of how Grace had told me in the cafe in Alcaster how he still had a way of bringing his troubles to her, as his elder sister, as he had when he was a child. But she had folded her hands in her lap and with her heavy eyebrows drawn together was staring down at them.

Martin looked at Luke, who suddenly became engrossed in studying Vanessa's profile.

"Well, hell," Martin said, seeing no help was coming from either of them, "what ought I to do? If I give myself up, it'll involve Grace and Luke as well, as they realize, because they helped me to conceal a death."

"I suppose that's what you were trying to think out, sitting in the Station Hotel," Peter said.

"Just so," Martin said. "And I don't really think there's anything I can do but give myself up to the police, as they're almost certain to identify the skeleton, if they haven't already."

"I agree with you," Henrietta said. "There'll be a trial, of course, and a scandal, but with luck your reputation may survive it. People are much more liberal-minded, if that's the word I want, though I don't believe it is, about such misdemeanours than they were even twenty years ago. You've got your witnesses that it wasn't murder, and you haven't tried to defraud anyone in any way, so you may get off with nothing but a few stern words from the judge about your incredible folly—with which I shall concur.

Honestly, Martin, how could you ever be such an unutterable fool?"

"That's what I've often asked myself," he said. "I always hated going into the house, you know. That's why I didn't come to see you more often than I did. It was nothing to do with my feelings for you."

"I'm glad to hear it," she said drily. She turned to Beryl. "I suppose you were too young to know anything about all this."

"Yes, I think I must have been away at school," Beryl answered, "and Peter was at Oxford."

I said, "At least I think Martin's cleared himself of having started the fire. Of all the people here, he's got the least motive for doing it. Peter, I think we might go home now. I've a good deal of work to do today."

"Thank you, Freda," Martin said. "You know, I've had a feeling ever since we met that you and I could understand each other better than most people. Of course you're quite right, I didn't start the fire. It's the last thing I'd have wanted."

Peter did not seem to want to move.

"Martin, if you're really going to the police," he said, "shall I go with you? If you'd like some moral support, that's to say. I know I'm no use as a witness."

"Nice of you," Martin said. "I appreciate it. But I'm still not dead sure of what I mean to do." He paused and looked round at everyone there. "I take it that everything that's been said in this room can be kept in the family for the present. Is that right?"

The answer was silence, which he seemed to accept as agreement.

"Well, when I've made up my mind what to do, I'll tell you," he said. "And if I go to the police, there'll be no need for them to know that this conversation ever took place. I'll need Grace and Luke as witnesses that I didn't commit murder, but the rest of you can remain in a state of total ignorance, which will be far the most convenient for you. Family loyalty is a splendid thing, isn't it? I can count on you and you can count on me."

He smiled at his audience, once more completely in command of the situation.

On my way home with Peter, my thoughts went back to the discussion I had had with him while we were standing looking at the burnt-out shell of Henrietta's house, the discussion on the subject of loyalty. I had assumed then that he had been thinking of his loyalty to Simon, wondering if there had been any virtue in it, yet now it seemed just as likely that he had been thinking about some member of his family and that feelings far deeper than those he had had for Simon had been involved. Was he sure that someone in the family had set fire to the house and had he a suspicion, right or wrong, of which of them it could be?

However, as we walked home I started to think once more about my afternoon's work, and as Peter was as disinclined to talk as I was, we reached home without having exchanged more than a few casual words. Over our usual lunch of sandwiches Peter read the newspaper, then went upstairs and the sound of his typewriter reached me as I got to work in the kitchen on the canapés I had undertaken to make for the party that evening.

I became so engrossed in this that it was some time before I noticed that the typewriter had once more become silent, and when I did, I thought it was hardly surprising that Peter should be unable to concentrate on the cerebration of the mild little Oxford don who sidled timidly through all the books that he had written so far, but of whom he now said that he was desperately tired, when he had so many other calamities to think about. I went on with my own work and about five o'clock loaded the van and drove off to make a delivery of what I had made. When I reached home again I did not bother to put the van into the garage, but left it standing outside it, and went indoors, where I found that Peter had come downstairs and was waiting for me in the living-room. I started to ask him how his afternoon's work had gone, but he made an impatient gesture and said, "Listen, I've got to tell you something."

"In that case, let's have some sherry," I said. "It's very cold outside. I'm frozen."

He poured out drinks for us both and we settled down in our usual chairs on either side of the fire.

"I've been a fool," he said, "and now I don't know what to do about it."

"Like Martin?" I suggested.

"Nothing as serious as that, but I ought to have told you about it straight away—I nearly did the other night—but then I thought of how you'd always disliked Simon, so I kept it to myself. But now he's dead there's no point in doing that any longer, and I think I'd better tell you the whole thing."

I remembered that when we had been in bed in the night after the fire he had asked me what I would think if he had done something really stupid, something, moreover, that could not be undone. But somehow we had started to talk of other things and he had never told me what it was.

"Well, go on," I said.

"Those damned Bullers—or rather, those damned fakes," he said, "I stole them."

"You *what?*" I stared at him incredulously. "You!"

He nodded despondently.

"For heaven's sake, why?" I asked.

"It was because of that man Baynes coming down to look at them," he said. "I'd always been fairly certain they were fakes and that Simon had produced them. I didn't know how he got them into Max's hands till Max told us about that meeting in London and the antique shop in Brighton, but, as I've told you, I'd been to Simon's studio and seen some fakes he'd done, one or two Bullers among them. And there was something about that yew tree in the picture of the church that always worried me—I don't know if you ever noticed it, but it was exactly the same as that tree is now. I didn't think that could be right. I know yews grow very slowly and last for hundreds of years, but I thought it must have grown a bit, or been lopped or something, since the time Buller was supposed to have painted it. So I was suspicious from the start."

"But you let Henrietta go on thinking the pictures were genuine," I said.

"Well, they gave her a lot of pleasure, didn't they? I didn't see why I should spoil that."

"And you stole them to protect Simon before the expert got here."

"That was my idea."

"Where are they now?"

"Under some sacks in the garage."

"*Our* garage?"

"Yes. And I don't know what to do with them now. You see, when I took them I naturally didn't know there was going to be a fire. I thought I'd just take them and keep them out of the way till Everett Baynes had gone back to America, then I'd let them turn up in somebody's barn or somewhere. That's actually happened with far more valuable paintings than the Bullers. I believe it's because the thieves who take them think they can hold them up to ransom and that they'll be paid out of the insurance money, then they make the horrid discovery that the pictures aren't insured at all because no one can afford to pay the premiums, so they just abandon them. Well, I thought I could arrange something like that and Henrietta would get them back all right and wouldn't need to sell them again because Martin and the rest of us were going to chip in to boost her income. And I went out in the evening after Henrietta's party and got the things and hid them in the garage. You didn't hear me go out because you'd fallen asleep in here and I got back without your ever knowing I'd been away. It was quite easy getting in and out of the house, because they never kept it locked up in the daytime, and Henrietta was lying down and Beryl, I suppose, was in the kitchen. If she'd come out, it wouldn't have surprised her very much to see me. I could have made up some yarn to account for it. But then the house went on fire and of course everyone assumed the Bullers went up in smoke. And as I said, I nearly told you all about it that evening, but then, thinking how much you disliked Simon, I assumed you'd only tell me what a fool I'd been—as of course, I had—and I didn't feel like being told so at that time of night."

"So now you've got the fake Bullers on your hands and you don't know what to do with them."

"Yes, that's the position."

I thought it over as seriously as I could, but the trouble was I wanted to laugh.

"How certain are you they're fakes?" I asked.

"About a hundred per cent."

"Because if there's any chance they're genuine, I think I'd simply give them back to Henrietta and tell her the whole story. She'd probably be amused."

"I thought of that, but if I'm right that they're fakes and she found out I'd always known they were, she wouldn't be very pleased with me, would she? And getting them back wouldn't give her any pleasure."

"Then why not let them really go up in smoke? Let's have a quiet bonfire in the garden and burn them."

"I suppose because I've got just a little scrap of fear that in spite of all the evidence, they might be genuine, and once I'd burnt them I'd become more and more certain they were."

"Then I think the best thing to do would be what you meant to do originally and let them turn up somewhere so that Henrietta gets them back, then she can do what she wants with them. If she gets another expert to look at them and she's told by him they're fakes, she needn't know you ever had any doubts of them, and—well, it can't hurt Simon now, can it, if he's found out? And she just might go on liking them as much as before. It could be she likes them for themselves and not just because they're by a moderately famous painter. Simon himself was rather proud of them, wasn't he? I think he rather wanted to tell us they were his work. Peter . . ."

"Yes?"

"D'you think that's why he was on the spot when the house was set alight? If we're right that he was and that's how he saw who did it, did he go there to try to steal the pictures because we'd told him Everett Baynes was coming?"

*

"I've wondered about that myself," Peter said. "He might actually have got into the house a little while after I did and found they were missing already. He'd have got a kick out of that, thinking that someone had thought them worth stealing. But even if he didn't do that, he could at least have been in the garden, close to the garage, and seen quite clearly who set the fire going."

"It all hangs together, doesn't it?"

"Except that we still haven't managed to come up with any kind of motive for anyone to have wanted to burn the house down."

"No."

Peter got up and refilled our glasses and we sat quietly, sipping our sherry, while I thought that I really ought to be doing something about supper. There were the remains of yesterday's stew, which I could warm up, and there was some cheese. That would be the easiest. After a few minutes I went out to the kitchen, put the stew on the stove and switched on the ring under it at its lowest, so that it would take some time to warm up. I was in no hurry to eat.

There were still one or two things I wanted to talk over while Peter was in a talking mood.

Returning to the living-room, I sat down again and said, "Peter, has Max always known those pictures were fakes? Could he have been in it with Simon?"

I saw that he had considered this before, but he only said, "How nice we're becoming about all our friends, aren't we? We'll be suspecting each other soon."

"But could he?"

"I suppose it's possible. There wouldn't have been a great deal of money for either of them if they had to share it, but still they might have thought it was worth while. But are you really asking if I think Max might have burnt the house down as a way of getting rid of the pictures before Everett Baynes could see them?"

"Well, do you?"

"No, I don't."

"I agree it sounds a bit fantastic, but I'm just trying to think of every possibility."

"You've got to remember Max rescued Henrietta from the fire. Really he risked his own life to do it."

"But mightn't he be capable of burning the house down to destroy the pictures, yet not have had any intention of committing murder? When he saw Henrietta at the window, perhaps he couldn't bring himself to walk away, leaving her to roast to death."

"But somebody did." As he said this, Peter gave me a startled look, as if he had just said something that had taken him by surprise. "Yes," he muttered, "somebody did."

I went on to say that I was sure there was nothing in the case that I had just tried to make against Max, and that I was glad of it because I had always liked him, but Peter did not answer. He did not answer when I made one or two other remarks. He appeared abruptly to have withdrawn into one of his silences. I knew the look on his face, absent and brooding. To go on trying to talk to him would be a waste of effort.

It depressed me, partly because I felt that something that one of us had said in the last few minutes must have provoked his change of mood, and partly because it seemed to me that the last thing we wanted just then was a sense of separateness. If we could not talk freely to one another, thoughts bottled up inside the two of us could only too easily become ugly and distorted. Uglier even than the truth on which one of us, or more probably Superintendent Beddowes, might stumble at any time.

I suddenly felt that I was in danger of losing my temper with Peter. It was a longish time since I had done so, and all at once I felt that after the tension of the last two days it would be an unutterable relief to stamp, shout, swear and yell at him that he had no right, now of all times, to behave as if I were not there in the room with him. In the early days of our marriage I would probably have made a scene, but experience had made me cautious. I knew that in the end, if I let myself go, it would be me who got hurt. If I could keep my patience and turn my attention to something else, Peter would emerge from the hiding-place that he went to on such occasions and behave as if nothing in the least out of the ordinary had happened. I finished my sherry, got up and started towards the kitchen to dish up the supper.

Then all of a sudden I rushed forward and flung open the kitchen door. I could smell it. The wretched stew was burning.

But of course it was not. Absurdly, I had made the same mistake as before, and as before I had known that, even though my first automatic action was to shoot across the kitchen to the stove and snatch the saucepan off it. My next action was to tear open the back door and race out into the garden. Peter was at my heels and as I hesitated for a moment, blind in the sudden darkness, he passed me and ran to the garage.

Unlike Henrietta's, it was not attached to the house. It had been built by my father and was of brick, with a shingle roof. It had no window, but it had a door that slid upwards, and because I had not put the van away inside it when I returned from delivering my order that evening, it was now open and thick smoke was billowing out of it into the night. I could see the smoke which was enveloping the van as it stood in front of the garage because there was a flickering of flame inside which filled it with a wavering red light. There was not actually much fire yet. A heap of stuff that looked like newspapers and sacks had been set alight on the concrete floor and flames were licking through it, but unless they reached the roof, they were not likely to do much damage.

But Peter, ahead of me, shouted, "Move the van! It may catch where it is. I'll deal with this."

He plunged into the garage, which happened also to be the garden shed and contained the garden tools, and dodging past the burning heap, he dragged out the rolled up garden hose and pulled it towards the stand-pipe just outside the garage, plugged the hose in, turned on the tap and started a spray of water on to the fire.

Meanwhile I had clambered into the driving-seat of the van, switched on the lights, started the engine and was just about to back the van towards the gate when I became aware of two figures rolling on the ground in a violent struggle. They had been invisible in the shadow of the van until I had turned on the lights, but the moment I did so one of them began to scream and at the same time seemed to collapse under the weight of the other, lying shaking and twitching and filling the night with the meaningless shrieking of hysteria. It was Ilse Klein. The other figure was a man, but as he crouched over the woman, pinning her to the ground, I did not immediately recognize him. Then he stood up and turned towards me, and I saw it was Max Ormerod.

"Come here, can you, Freda?" he said. "I don't know what to do with her."

I backed the van a little way away from the garage, clambered down and joined Max beside the woman on the ground. Her shrieking and shaking had suddenly stopped and she lay there limply with her eyes closed. I doubted if she was conscious.

"We'd better get her inside," I said, "and get the doctor."

"The doctor—not the police?" Max said. He was breathing hard, his hair had tumbled over his forehead, he had a scratch, which was bleeding, down one thin cheek, and he had lost his glasses.

That was the first thing that I noticed. "Your glasses, Max—where are they?"

"They're somewhere around," he answered, putting a hand up vaguely to his eyes. "If you could find them . . . I'm rather helpless without them."

I stooped and started looking for them on the ground around our feet and after a moment found them and gave them to Max.

Putting them on, he said, "Now if you can help me to lift her . . ."

"I think I'd better get Peter," I said. "You two can carry her in and I'll look after the fire."

I went to the garage and took the hose from Peter, while he went to where Ilse lay on the ground and together with Max, lifted her and carried her into the cottage.

The spray from the hose, hissing on the flames, had already reduced the fire and after a minute or two I ventured past it to fetch a rake from the back of the garage and use it to beat at the burning heap and spread it out on the concrete so that the water would more easily reach the remaining flames. I saw that at the centre of the pile there was a small tin which I supposed had contained petrol or paraffin and that newspapers, as well as rubbish which I recognized as a collection of sacks and other old things that Peter and I had allowed to accumulate in the garage, had been stacked on top of the tin. And in the litter I saw what was without question the charred remnants of Henrietta's pictures, whether by Francis Buller or Simon Edge, of her old home and of the village church.

Sardonically, I thought, "Well, that's one problem solved."

Nothing whatever need be said about them now.

Beating out the last sparks of the fire with the rake and giving the ashes one more drenching with the hose, I turned the water off at the stand-pipe and went into the cottage.

Ilse Klein lay on the sofa, white and limp and with her eyes still closed. Peter had put a cushion under her head and covered her with a blanket. Max was standing by the fire, mopping at the bleeding scratch on his face and holding a large glass of whisky.

"I've phoned Roger," Peter said. "He says he can be here in a few minutes."

Roger Ellison was the doctor who had taken over Edmund Kenworthy's practice in Alcaster, and who, like him, lived and had a surgery in the village.

"You seem to have an almost miraculous gift of being on the spot when you're needed, Max," I said. "How do you manage it?"

"Well, this time it wasn't entirely an accident," he said. "I'd a feeling something like this might be going to happen, so I came along."

"What d'you mean, you'd a feeling it might happen?" I asked. "You don't mean . . ." I paused as I thought it out. "You don't mean you *knew* she was our incendiary?"

His face gave one of its sharp twitches. "I did, as a matter of fact."

"And you said nothing about it?"

"Well, I was sorry for her, you see," he said. "She's had such a rotten life, it's no wonder she's gone a bit peculiar. That business of having to leave your home and your country and the work you were good at—I'm not sure if anyone of our age can really take in how terrible it was—and then, on top of that, to get that awful arthritis in her hands, so that she couldn't even play the piano for her own pleasure. So we talked it over and I thought I'd got her to understand how desperately dangerous it was for her to go on as she was doing, and she promised she'd never do it again. I think something must have upset her recently to set her going once more."

"I think I upset her today," Peter said, "by telling the police Simon had a phone call yesterday afternoon from a woman with a foreign accent. They seem to have gone straight round to see Ilse and questioned her about it. So I suppose this affair tonight was revenge."

"How did you find out about her, Max?" I asked.

"I just happened to catch her at it," he answered. "I was in the shed at the dig one evening when I heard someone prowling around outside and there she was with her little can of petrol and some sticks and things, piling them up against the wall of the shed. It's just wood, so if she'd got a fire started it would have gone up like a torch. But she broke down after I caught her and confessed she'd lit all the other fires that have happened around here, and as I said, she promised she'd never do it again. I suppose it was stupid of me to believe her. People like her can't help themselves, but when she's lucid she's an intelligent woman. And somehow I couldn't bring myself to go to the police, as I suppose I should have done. I was just too sorry for her."

"But how did you guess she'd try again tonight?" I asked.

"I was just driving home from the dig," he said, "and I

saw her in that awful little car of hers at the crossroads, turning down this lane. And so far as I know she hardly ever goes out at night, so I got a feeling that if she was out, it just could mean mischief. After all, there was Henrietta's fire . . ." His face twitched again. "I know I ought to have gone to the police after that. I've been telling myself over and over again I ought to go, but still—well, it seemed so brutal. All the other fires she's lit have been like the one she lit tonight in your garage, not really dangerous to anyone, but with Henrietta's it was different. So I'll have to do something, I know I shall. You think I ought to, don't you?"

There was a little cough from the sofa.

The three of us turned quickly to look at Ilse. Her eyes were open and there was a mocking light in them.

"You may do as you please, Mr. Ormerod," she said. "You have been kind to me and I appreciate it. And I am sorry I broke my promise to you tonight. But I did not set fire to Mrs. Cosgrove's house. If I am touched in the head, I am not a murderer. And I can prove it. I have an alibi. That surprises you, doesn't it? It is true I do not go out in the evenings. Nearly always I am alone with no one to say where I am. Only once or twice I ever go out. But that night is one time when I did, because I needed the pills for the pain in my hands. So I went to Dr. Ellison's surgery and there I wait one hour, two hours, I lose count of the time, because he is delayed, and so his receptionist will tell you."

CHAPTER 8

Roger Ellison arrived a few minutes later. He was a short, heavily built man of about fifty-five with a pink, somewhat puffy face and a broad, bald forehead.

"Now what's all this, Miss Klein?" he asked in a tone of friendly interest. "You've been trying to set fire to Mr. Cosgrove's garage? That was very, very wrong of you."

Though his tone was almost jocular, his eyes on Ilse Klein's pale face were warily observant.

"They tell you this?" she said. "You believe them?" Then she gave a little giggle. "Yes, you believe them and I will not pretend it is not true. There are too many against me. There have always been too many against me. Even when I have been a child, they do not believe me when I tell them the beautiful thoughts I have in my mind. They tell me not to lie. 'You are a little liar, Ilse,' they say, even my good mother and father, 'we can never believe you.' So I lock the thoughts up in my head and speak of them only when I am alone, so when someone overhears me, he says, 'She speaks to herself, she is mad.' You think I am mad, Dr. Ellison, isn't it? You want to lock me up."

He drew a chair up beside the sofa on which she was lying.

"Well, we can't have you going around the countryside, setting things on fire, can we?" he said. "We'll have to tell the police about it, shan't we?"

She gave another little giggle. "And they will lock me up," she said, almost with satisfaction, as if she rather enjoyed the prospect. It made me wonder if somewhere at the back of the woman's sick mind there was a longing to hand herself over to people who would take care of her, be responsible for her and to whom her symptoms would make her important.

She went on, "But I did not set fire to Mrs. Cosgrove's house. You know that, Dr. Ellison. I was sitting in your surgery, waiting for you, all the time everyone else in Ickfield was running to see the fire."

He looked up at Peter. "That's perfectly true. There was a bad pile-up on the London road, just outside Alcaster. A lorry, a sports car and a motor cycle. One man killed and two badly injured and the lorry driver, who was responsible for the whole thing, going out of his mind with shock. I was called to it and I was more than an hour late for the surgery. I saw the fire from the crossroads, and the people streaming to look at it, but I went straight home and found Miss Klein waiting for me and my receptionist told me she'd been there since the surgery opened."

"Correct," she said. "I am not to blame for that fire."

He looked back at her. "But what are we going to do with you?"

"I will go home," she said. "I am now perfectly well. If Mr. Ormerod had not attacked me, I would not have fainted. I am very well, thank you. I will go home."

"I'm sorry, but I don't think we can let you do that," Roger said. "I think, you know, the best thing will be to take you along to St. Brigid's. You can spend the night quietly there, and I'll tell the police where you are and they'll probably be along to see you in the morning."

St. Brigid's was a mental hospital near Alcaster, a small place but with a good reputation.

Ilse Klein's face went expressionless as he spoke, then she opened her mouth and looked as if she had decided to start screaming again. But instead she slowly closed her mouth, closed her eyes for a moment, opened them, smiled faintly and said, "Very well, doctor, I do as you say. I shall be a good girl now."

Throwing off the blanket with which Peter had covered her, she tried to get to her feet. Roger moved swiftly and caught her. If he had not done so, she would have fallen to the floor, for she seemed to have no strength in her legs. As he held her, she began to giggle again and she was still chuckling to herself as Roger, with Peter's help, half-carried her out of the cottage and out to his car.

Her own car was still in the lane. To get it off the road, Peter drove it in at the gate, then before returning to the living-room, drove the van into the garage and pulled the door shut. When he came into the room he was holding a small bundle of charred material which I recognized as the remnants of the two Francis Bullers. He took the bundle straight to the kitchen and I heard him open the back door and the clang of the dustbin lid as he pushed it into it.

Max had fidgeted about the room while Peter was gone, but when he returned, stood still and said unhappily, "I wish she hadn't got to be handed over to the police. It doesn't seem the right thing to do with someone like her."

Peter gave him an absent look, as if he had not taken in what Max had said. I saw that now that the excitement of the fire was over he had once more returned into one of his silences, brooding on I did not know what, but I had a feeling that it was not Ilse Klein.

"I shouldn't think she'd ever have to stand trial," I said. "The medicals will say she isn't fit to plead."

"And they'll keep her in St. Brigid's?" Max said.

"For a time, wouldn't you think?" I answered. "For her own safety it'll probably be the best thing. When the news of what she's been doing gets around, she isn't going to be exactly popular."

"No." He gave another dab at his cheek with his handkerchief, looked at it and saw that the scratch had stopped bleeding. "It's what ought to have happened to her when I caught her out at the dig. I'm to blame for this affair to-night. I'm sorry about it."

I shook my head. "Don't be. I expect we'd have done what you did if it hadn't happened to Henrietta's house. That somehow gave the whole thing a new dimension."

"But she'd nothing to do with that," Max said.

"Only we didn't know that till we heard her alibi. I know when I saw the fire in our garage and you struggling with her on the ground, I took for granted we'd caught our fire-raiser."

"Whereas he's still to be discovered. You don't think . . . ?"

"Yes?" I said as he paused.

"Oh, nothing. It would be easier to guess who it is if we knew of anyone who had a grudge against Henrietta, and there may be someone who has one. Her tongue's quite sharp now and then. Well, good night. I hope nothing more untoward happens this evening."

"Just a minute, Max," Peter said suddenly. He was half turned away from Max and did not look at him as he spoke, but frowned at a spot on the floor at his feet. "I suppose by now you've told the police that the cupboard was there when my father bought the house."

Max shifted from one foot to the other, looking embarrassed. "No, they haven't been along to see me again," he answered.

"But you do remember the cupboard, don't you?"

Max's embarrassment seemed to deepen. "As a matter of fact, I've been wanting to talk to you about it. I haven't been able to make up my mind what to do."

"I don't see what your problem is. It doesn't involve you."

"Well, in a way it does. For one thing, you're my friends and I don't want to make trouble for you all. For another thing . . ."

Peter turned his head and looked at him. "Yes?"

"I didn't really mean to talk about it now," Max said. "I mean, it doesn't seem the right time to talk about one's own affairs. But there's a possibility, you see, that I may be joining the Cosgrove clan. Beryl and I have been talking about getting married."

Peter stared at him for a moment, then burst out laughing. It was laughter of a kind that troubled me, I was not sure why. I only felt there was something harsh in it, something almost cruel and not like Peter.

"So you've got around to it at last," he said. "I've often wondered if you ever would."

"Oh, we haven't really made up our minds about it," Max said quickly. "It's just something we've been discussing."

"That sounds very passionate."

Max flushed. "We're neither of us as young as we were. We thought you might find it ridiculous."

"It's never too late to get married," Peter said. "My own father went on doing it into his old age."

"I'm so very glad to hear it, Max," I said and went up to him and kissed him. "And Henrietta will be too. She's always hoped Beryl would get married sooner or later. Or have you told her about it already?"

"We haven't told anyone," Max replied. "I've wanted to marry Beryl for some time, but she's had doubts about it. She's always said things were so good between us as they were, we were such good friends and worked together so well, there wasn't any need to make any change and that getting married might not suit us at all. But I think I've managed to change her mind for her. Henrietta's birthday had something to do with it. Beryl faced the fact that at eighty you can't expect to live for ever and that when Henrietta dies, she'll be all alone. And she knew Henrietta would be glad about it."

"This is the first time I've ever heard of anyone getting married to please her stepmother," Peter said. "The thought of that doesn't offend you?"

"For God's sake, Peter, why have you got to go all sarcastic all of a sudden?" I exclaimed. "Why don't you tell Max you're delighted to welcome him into what he calls the Cosgrove clan? I thought this was the sort of occasion when men shake hands and slap each other on the back and make self-conscious congratulatory noises. Speaking as an honorary member of the clan myself, Max, I'm delighted."

"But of course I am too," Peter said, "particularly if it helps you to forget that cupboard."

"We'd better talk about that," Max said, and abandoning his intention of leaving, sat down and pressing his hands together, began kneading them nervously together. "Is it the best thing to do? As I told you, I took care to say nothing to the police that I couldn't unsay. I mean, I said I was only fifteen or thereabouts when my mother and I moved out of the house and I don't remember there ever being a cupboard on the landing. But if you think that's a mistake, I could always say I seem to remember there was a toy-cupboard there when I was a kid. Or I could go on just leaving it vague, couldn't I, if you see what I mean?"

"Do you think you can go on getting away with it?" Peter asked.

"I don't see why not."

"And you'd do that to help Martin? You know it's Martin you'd be helping, don't you? I suppose Beryl's told you that."

"Well, of course, Martin himself doesn't mean anything to me," Max said. "But Beryl does, and it's what she wants me to say. She came into my office this afternoon and told me all about Martin's confession and how the rest of them are involved. And she thinks if the police can't date the time when the cupboard was papered over, they're unlikely to be able to make any positive identification of the skeleton, and that would get Martin off the hook."

"And would save you from marrying into a family with a criminal record."

"Look," Max said with exasperation, "that isn't why I'm suggesting it. I thought you'd be pleased if I took the line Beryl wants. And apart from her, you two and Grace and Henrietta are old friends of mine and I don't mind stretching the truth a little to help you all. But if you don't want me to do that, I'll go straight to the police and tell them my memory's cleared and I'm certain there was a cupboard in the passage where I kept my old toys, but that there was no skeleton there in my time."

Peter nodded thoughtfully. "I'm sorry, Max. Don't think I'm ungrateful. But let's think this thing out. I can foresee complications ahead."

"Such as?"

"Nothing specific, but there are always dangers when one deviates from the truth."

Max stood up, preparing once more to leave. "I suppose it couldn't be that you don't want Martin to get off the hook," he said. "The two of you haven't been the most devoted of brothers, so Beryl's told me."

"The odd thing is, I'm really trying to work out what would be best for him," Peter answered, "and so I'd like to have a little time to think."

"All right, but try not to take too long about it." Max said it sharply, but then all of a sudden his face lit up with a smile. "You know, I'm glad I told you about Beryl and me. It makes it seem more real. It was probably quite the wrong time to do it—you've got so much to worry about. All the same, I'm glad I did. And I'll say whatever you like about the cupboard."

He went quickly to the door and let himself out.

As it closed behind him, Peter flung himself down in a

chair, leant back, thrusting his hands deep into his pockets, and stared at the fire. I felt very annoyed with him. He had not taken the news of his sister's coming marriage to Max at all as I thought he should. I could see too that now that Max had gone, Peter had relapsed into the mood which had possessed him before the discovery of the fire and of Ilse Klein. So whatever had precipitated it, it had been nothing said by Max but might have been something said by me, or even himself.

I knew how easily, and often how mistakenly, I blamed myself for Peter's bad moods. I knew too that even if occasionally I was responsible for causing one, however unintentionally, nothing that I could do would ever affect its duration. It would go as unpredictably as it had come. So at the moment the best thing to do would be to go to the kitchen and reheat the stew. All the same, as I left him, I wished I could remember just what we had been talking about when he showed the first symptoms of withdrawal.

It did not take long for the stew to warm up, but it was late and I was very tired, so instead of laying the table in the living-room, I dished the stew up on two plates, put them on a tray, added knives and forks, some bread and cheese, and carried the tray into the living-room, thinking that Peter and I would eat our supper sitting by the fire. But as I came through the door, I saw that Peter had left the room. I supposed he had gone upstairs. Putting the tray down on a table, I went to the bottom of the stairs and called out, "Peter!"

There was no answer and after a moment I called again. When there was still no answer I went upstairs and looked into his workroom, our bedroom, the bathroom and even the small room where Simon had slept. Peter was not in any of them. In fact, he was not in the cottage. Some time while I had been busy with the supper, he had quietly got up and left.

It scared me. He could be morose, but he was seldom inconsiderate. If he had done such a thing, it was because he had something on his mind so upsetting, perhaps so threatening, so frightening, that he had not been able to bring himself to speak of it at all, even to tell me that he wanted to go out for a while. Because I was scared it did not occur to me to be angry. I ate my plateful of stew without any appetite, did not bother with the cheese, and carried the tray out to the kitchen again. I found myself listening with deepening anxiety for the sound of his footsteps on the garden path. The time seemed to pass very slowly and the silence outside to grow increasingly ominous.

Then it was not footsteps that I heard, but the rattle of Ilse Klein's little car, or that was what I supposed it was when I heard it turn in at the gate and stop in front of the cottage. Peter must have taken it when he left because, having left it where he had, he would not have been able to get the van past it. A moment later I heard voices, one Peter's and the other, to my surprise, Henrietta's. It seemed extraordinarily late for Henrietta to be out. I glanced at my watch. It was only eight o'clock, not late at all, and it meant that Peter had been gone for only about twenty minutes.

He opened the door and Henrietta came into the room. She was wearing the sheepskin jacket that I had lent her and stood blinking in the light, looking bewildered and a little frightened.

"Well, I'm here," she said. "I don't understand it, but Peter wouldn't explain. I was just going to bed when he came. I didn't want any supper, I'd just had a hot drink, and he came straight upstairs to my room and he didn't want me even to tell the others I was coming out with him. They'd all gone into the dining-room, so I was able to leave without anyone knowing. I don't understand it, but he isn't a fool, so I suppose he's got his reasons."

He steered her to a chair by the fire.

"I've got you away from that house," he said. "That was the main thing."

"But why?" she said. "What's wrong with it? What's happened? What's the matter?"

He sat down beside her, reached for her hand and held it. His mood had altered. He was affectionate and gentle.

"I don't much want to talk about it yet," he said. "D'you think you could take it on trust for a little while that it was a good thing to do?"

"That's asking a good deal."

"It's just that I could be wrong."

The look she gave him was penetrating. "I believe you've got it into your head I'm in some danger in that house. Isn't that a little ridiculous?"

"Is it?" he said. "You had a very narrow squeak the other night. If Max hadn't rescued you, you wouldn't have come out alive."

"And you really think that's what someone intended and that someone's a Cosgrove and may mean to have another go at me."

She sounded astonishingly calm about it, as if the thought were not an entirely new one to her.

Peter hesitated. "I said I may be wrong."

I said, "Are you staying the night, Henrietta, because if you are I'll go and get your room ready for you? You must be very tired."

"I believe I'm staying," Henrietta answered. "I think that was Peter's intention when he brought me here."

"Oh yes, certainly," he said. "And I must say, you're bearing up very well under the strain of being kidnapped."

"Well, get me some whisky," she said. "I'm afraid I've got through a good deal of yours already, but it does help at a time like this. Then I'll go to bed. You're right, Freda, I'm very tired. Tired and muddled. You do understand, don't you, Peter, that the only member of your family who stands to benefit by my death is your sister Beryl?"

"Yes," he said, "I see that."

"I'd left her the house, so if I'd died she'd have got the insurance at once, and I suppose that'll be seventy thousand or thereabouts. But if I live to be ninety or whatever, she'll have to wait quite a long time for her inheritance, as Martin remarked at our lunch party."

"But that's nonsense," I said. "She couldn't have murdered Simon. She was with you yourself at the time he was killed."

Henrietta smiled at me. "I'm glad you remembered that. It's just what I was going to say myself. And I don't suppose for a moment Peter's forgotten it, so he's got some other suspect in mind. But I'll wait till the morning when I can think a bit more clearly myself than I can now to find out who it is. Thank you—" She reached for the whisky that Peter had just poured out for her. "Are you going to lend me a night-dress again, Freda? When all these troubles are over I'll buy you a nice new one to show my appreciation. But d'you know, one could get to like wandering about like this without any luggage. One feels very free, very comfortably irresponsible. Nothing heavy to carry, nothing to worry about losing. How much of the troubles of one's life come from fretting about one's possessions."

She was trying to speak with her usual cheerfulness, but I thought that I had never seen her look so exhausted, so close to a breaking point. Unless Peter had some very good reason for having spirited her away from Grace's house, he was much to be blamed. Going upstairs, I made up the bed in the spare bedroom once more, put a hot-water bottle into it and laid out one of my night-dresses on it. When I went downstairs again, I found Peter telling Henrietta about the fire that evening in our garage and the discovery that it was Ilse Klein who had been lighting the fires that had disturbed the neighbourhood during the last few months.

"But she didn't set fire to your house, you see, Henrietta," he said, "because she'd a perfect alibi. All the same, it seems to me that someone probably thought of doing it because he knew we'd a pyromaniac at large and thought he could count on her being blamed. It was just his bad luck that she went to see Ellison that evening."

"Yes—well, we'll talk it over tomorrow," Henrietta said. "But will you telephone Grace and tell her I'm here? Even if she's your suspect, I shouldn't like her to worry unnecessarily when she finds I'm missing." She started to get up. But as she did so she swayed and if she had not been able to catch at Peter's arm, would have fallen. "Oh dear, I oughtn't to have had that whisky," she said. "Perhaps you'd help me upstairs, Freda. I'm sorry to be such a nuisance."

I put an arm round her and supported her up the stairs. Then I stayed in the bedroom in case she needed any help getting undressed, but she managed it by herself, pulled my night-dress on over her head and climbed into the bed. Lying back on the pillows, she gave a little sigh of relief at being able to relax. Her grey eyes had a cloudy look and seemed to have some difficulty in focussing on my face.

"Peter isn't a fool, you know," she said. "Perhaps you'd tell him, I do trust him."

She closed her eyes.

I watched her for a moment in case she wanted to say something more, but as she was silent I went out, closing the door softly behind me.

*

Going swiftly downstairs, I turned on Peter.

"For God's sake, what did you think you were doing, bringing her out like this?" I demanded. "She's near to collapse. She's too old for this kind of thing."

"Well, something had to be done," he answered. "We couldn't risk leaving her in that house."

"I don't understand why."

"For the reason I told her. Someone tried to kill her in the fire and was liable to try again."

"What put that into your head?"

"You did. Didn't you say Max might have set the house on fire, but perhaps couldn't bring himself to let Henrietta roast to death?"

"And you said somebody did."

"Exactly."

I looked at him curiously. "Is that what you've been brooding about all this evening?"

"Have I been brooding? I'm sorry, I didn't mean to." He gave me an apologetic smile. "It's just that I couldn't stop thinking about it. I mean, that the fire was meant as murder. It hadn't occurred to me till you said what you did. But if that's what it was, what ought I to do?" He flung himself down in a chair and gave a great yawn. "Is there anything to eat? I'm hungry."

"There's that damned stew that I've warmed up twice already," I answered. "Warming it up doesn't improve it, but I'll do it again, if you like."

"It's all right, I'll do it," he said and disappeared into the kitchen.

In a few minutes he returned with a plateful of stew which he forked into his mouth, standing on the hearthrug.

"That was nice," he said as he scraped the plate clean. "One of your better stews."

"Now are you going to telephone Grace?" I asked.

"Presently."

"Why not now? She may be going mad with worry if she's found out Henrietta's disappeared."

"Well, let her worry for a little. It may spark something off."

"So you don't really know what you're doing. You've simply removed Henrietta to see if it will start some kind of panic, without caring what it might do to her."

"No, it isn't as simple as that. The worst of it is, I think I know . . ." He paused and thrust his fingers through his hair as if that would help him to sort out the confusion in his brain.

In the momentary silence we heard quick footsteps on the garden path and the ringing of the doorbell.

Peter went to open the door. Beryl, in a new tweed coat that she must have bought in Alcaster the day before and with a scarf tied over her hair, stood outside.

She came in quickly, saying, "Isn't she here?" There was a touch of frenzy in her voice and she looked round the room wildly, as if she expected to find Henrietta hiding in a corner.

"Henrietta?" Peter said. "Yes, she's here. She's gone to bed."

"And she's all right?"

"What d'you mean, all right? She's very tired."

"But that's all? She isn't—queer?"

"She seemed to me just her usual self," he said.

"Thank God for that!" Beryl dropped into a chair and untied her headscarf, shaking loose her reddish hair, which was so like Peter's. "When we found out she'd gone, just vanished without a word to anyone, we couldn't help thinking—well, what would you have thought?"

"That she'd wandered out by herself and got lost, was that it? In other words, that she'd started wandering in her mind. I'm sorry about that. The fact is, I came and got her."

"You *what?*"

"I came and got her," he repeated. "In Ilse's car. You didn't really think she'd be able to walk as far as this, did you?"

"We didn't know what to think. I came here on the off-chance when we couldn't find her in the village. I went to the old house first, thinking she might have had an impulse to look at the ruins, then I thought I'd just call in here, in case you knew anything about her. I didn't really expect to find her. But whatever made you come and take her, Peter?"

"I thought she'd be better off with us, that's all," he said.

"You don't make sense."

"All right, I don't. Let's leave it at that for the moment, shall we?"

"But why couldn't you at least get her to tell us she was coming to you and save us some of this awful worry?"

"I thought we'd only get involved in an argument. I didn't think Grace would let her go without a fuss. I was going to ring her presently and tell her Henrietta was here."

Beryl took off her glasses, took a handkerchief from her handbag and gave them a polish, as if she wanted a little time to think over the meaning of his strange actions. Without the glasses, her short-sighted eyes looked vacant and expressionless, but as soon as she put them on again, her eyes became acute and rather hard.

"You're up to something, and I don't like it," she said. "To ring Grace *presently*—that was considerate, wasn't it?" She turned to me. "Do you understand what all this is about, Freda?"

I did not want to admit that I understood almost as little as Beryl about what Peter had done. The easiest way to avoid answering the question, I thought, would be to change the subject.

"Did you know Max was here this evening?" I asked. "Have you heard about our fire?"

For a moment I thought that Beryl did not intend to answer, but would go on trying to discover the reason for Peter's abduction of Henrietta. But then, as if the subject were not important, she said brusquely, "Yes, he telephoned me and told me about it, but I gather it wasn't anything serious." Her pale face reddened slightly. "I believe he also told you we've been talking of getting married. I wish he hadn't. We haven't made up our minds."

"And I was just getting set to congratulate you," I said, "but that would be premature, would it?"

Beryl smiled uncertainly. At the same time she began twisting the headscarf that she was holding into a tight rope between her hands. Her knuckles were white.

"I suppose it wouldn't, I suppose we'll go ahead with it. I wonder if he told you . . ." She dropped her eyes to her tense hands. "Did he tell you we've been lovers for two years?"

Peter and I exchanged astonished glances. Such a possibility had never occurred to me. Beryl saw our expressions and gave a harsh little laugh.

"I see he didn't," she said. "He's always very discreet. And you didn't think I had it in me. Nor did I. All the same, it happened. A mistake, I've often thought, and really my fault, because I'd begun to worry that I was getting old and still knew nothing about sex, and I wanted to know what it was that I was missing. But Max didn't really know a great deal about it either, so it's never been a tremendous success. I suppose we're neither of us much interested in it really, and I think we'd have dropped it if either of us had known how to do it without hurting the other. Because we're very fond of one another, you know, and get on so well in our day-to-day lives."

"But if that's all there is to it," I said, "why get married?"

"Well, you see, I'm pregnant."

Again Peter and I looked at one another, I in sheer surprise, Peter with an expression that puzzled me—it seemed suddenly so desperate. It was as if he could not bear what his sister had told him. Yet it seemed unlikely that it should disturb him much. I would have expected him even to be glad of it. Yet from the time Max had told us of the engagement, Peter had not reacted as I would have expected.

"Oh, you poor idiot," he muttered.

"I don't know about that," Beryl said defensively. "In some ways I'm rather glad about it. I mean, it's another chance to find out what I've been missing before it's too late. But it's true our first idea was that I should have an abortion, and perhaps that's what I'll still do, though somehow I don't like the thought of it. I'd sooner get married and have the baby, I think. Still, the fact is we haven't decided when or where, or where we're going to live, or how soon I should give up my job, or anything like that. And you're absolutely the first people to know about it."

"Henrietta doesn't know?" I asked.

Beryl shook her head. As she talked she had gradually stopped torturing her headscarf and her hands lay relaxed in her lap.

"Of course, I don't know if she guessed," she said. "If she did, she never said anything about it. But then she wouldn't. She'd never badger one with questions if she could see one didn't want to talk about a thing."

"Why didn't you tell her? She wouldn't have minded."

"I don't know. It was just the way I felt. I suppose it was because of my feeling that the whole thing had been a mistake. I wanted to get quite clear about what I meant to do before I talked to anybody."

"And you're quite sure now marriage is the right answer," I said. I found myself feeling very sorry for Beryl because it was clear that if she had satisfied her curiosity as to what sex was, she had not discovered love and knew that she had not. "Marriages on account of children don't always work out."

"Nor do the other sort necessarily," Beryl answered. "Think of Martin and Louise."

"That's something I'd sooner not do," I said. "Where did you and Max manage to meet?"

"In his office at the dig." Beryl gave her harsh laugh again. "Not the most comfortable place in the world, but fine and private."

"Were you there when Ilse Klein tried to set fire to it?" Peter asked. It was almost as if for the first time he felt interested in what his sister had told him and me about her pregnancy and probable marriage.

"No," Beryl said.

"Did he tell you about it?"

"Not till tonight. He and I haven't yet achieved the happy state of sharing all our thoughts, as I'm sure you and Freda have." She stood up and started tying her scarf over her hair once more. "Well, I'm glad I found Henrietta, but mind you take care of her. She's frailer than you may realize. She puts on such a good show when there are other people about that I don't think they understand how that heart attack of hers last year weakened her. Spiriting her away from Grace's house, as you did, and probably scaring the wits out of her, can't have done her any good. But on your head be it. Good night."

She let herself out of the cottage into the darkness of the garden.

For a little while after she had gone Peter and I were silent. I watched him, seeing the desperation that I had seen for a moment on his face when Beryl had told us that she was pregnant, once more return to it. He looked intensely unhappy. I waited to see if he would speak to me, then when he said nothing, remarked, "That was a nasty crack of Beryl's about us sharing all our thoughts. I know you've got something on your mind now, but I don't know what it is. Wouldn't it be a good thing if you told me about it?"

He brushed a hand across his face in the gesture he used when he wanted to smooth away the expression on it.

"I'm wondering why Beryl chose to tell us all that this evening," he said.

I did not believe it was really what he had on his mind.

"Well, she'd have to tell us sometime," I said. "Pregnancy isn't a thing one can hide indefinitely. You can't hide it in a cupboard and paper it over, as you can a skeleton."

"Yes, unless she decided on an abortion, she'd have to tell us sometime, so why not now? I see." It sounded as if he found this more significant than I had thought it. "Freda, if you like I'll tell you something I can't get out of my mind, yet it doesn't quite make sense. You know that voice on the telephone, the one with the foreign accent?"

"Yes, I know there's always been something about it that worried you."

"Well, for a moment, just at the first word, I thought it was Beryl's."

"Oh, now I understand . . ." I got up and went to his side, sat down on the arm of his chair and put an arm round him. He leant his head against my side, but he did not look up at me. "You're thinking that if Beryl made that call with her voice disguised, she set Simon up for the murder. But she couldn't have done the murder herself because Henrietta gave her an alibi. But now we know how intimate she and Max are, it looks as if they might have managed the thing together—Beryl making the phone call to get Simon out to the dig, I suppose with the promise of paying him some money, and Max doing the murder when he got there. And that would mean it was the two of them Simon was trying to blackmail, so he must have seen them set fire to the house and try to kill Henrietta."

"Yes, and they've even got a motive of sorts for doing that," Peter said. "If they're going to get married and have a child and Beryl's going to have to give up her job, they'll be fairly short of money, and the insurance on the house would come in very useful, but only if Henrietta was dead. But there's a rather important thing the matter with that argument. Max saved Henrietta's life."

I leant my cheek against the top of his head. "Then you

can stop worrying about it, can't you? As you said, it doesn't make sense."

"But the wretched girl's my sister," he said. "If she did have anything to do with it . . . No." He broke off with a sigh. "No, she can't have. Max saved Henrietta and that makes nonsense of the whole thing. But if she did, I shouldn't know what to do. A man doesn't have to give evidence against his wife, but I don't think that holds with a sister. Yet I care a lot about her, even if I don't show it much."

"Why not leave it to the police?"

"Oh, that's what I'll do in fact. I don't mean to go out of my way to help them convict a member of my family. But that doesn't mean I can stop thinking about it. For one thing, till we know who it was, Henrietta may still be in danger."

"Well, come to bed. I'm very tired."

We stood up, Peter as usual putting the fire-screen in front of the fire, and we went upstairs together, tiptoeing very quietly past the room in which Henrietta lay, so as not to disturb her.

I slept very deeply that night, but woke early. I lay still for a time, watching Peter as he lay with his face half-buried in the pillow, sound asleep, yet with a little frown on his forehead, as if his worries had pursued him through his dreams and were troubling him still. About eight o'clock I got up, put on my dressing-gown and slippers and went downstairs. I filled the kettle and switched it on, ground coffee and put it into the filter. As the water was dripping through it I made some toast and started to arrange a tray to take up to Henrietta. Before taking it up I poured out a cup of coffee for myself and perched on the edge of the table to drink it. Then I went upstairs with the tray, knocked gently on Henrietta's door, opened it and went in.

There had been no answer from her to my knock, and

there never would be. She was white and still. When I touched her she was cold. There was a look of unearthly peace about her. Sometime in the night she had been granted the wish that she had made when she blew out the candle on her birthday cake and had died a painless death.

CHAPTER 9

Roger Ellison said, "Her heart, of course. I've been expecting it."

"It was as bad as that, was it?" Peter said. "Did she know that herself?"

"Oh yes," Roger answered. "She was the kind of person to whom one told the truth. She knew she had to be careful. All the same, it might have lasted her for several years if—well, if she'd been able to go on taking things quietly."

"If it hadn't been for the fire, you mean, and having to escape by a window, and being abducted by me last night when she was already dead tired." Peter gave a groan. We were in the living-room, drinking some fresh coffee that I had just made. I had taken Roger upstairs when he arrived and left him alone in the room with Henrietta, then I had gone to the kitchen to make the coffee while Peter waited, moving restlessly about the room, for Roger to reappear. He had not stayed upstairs long. "I suppose . . ." Peter went on. "I suppose there's no doubt it *was* her heart."

Roger gave him a quick look. "Is there any reason why you think there might be?"

"No," Peter said uncertainly. "No, I don't think so. If you're sure."

"If there's anything on your mind, Peter," Roger said, "hadn't you better tell me?"

"No, I'm sure you're right." Peter brushed a hand across his face. "Bringing her here—it seemed a good idea at the time—but it may have been what finished her off. It could have been my fault."

"Just why *did* you bring her here when I suppose she was quite comfortably settled in with Grace?" Roger asked. "It seems an odd thing to have done."

"It was just an idea I had that she'd prefer being with us," Peter said. "Something she said—I forget what it was exactly."

Of course he was lying and I had a feeling that Roger suspected it. But if he did, he did not pursue the subject.

"I can't see any reason why I shouldn't sign a death certificate," he said. "And if you like I'll speak to that undertaker, Craven, and tell him to come here."

"That would be very kind of you," I said.

"And let me know if there's anything I can do. You'll probably want to get in touch with Grace yourself, or have you done that already?"

"No, but I'll telephone now," I said.

He went to the door, but hesitated there, looking at Peter. "You're sure there isn't something you want to tell me?"

Peter, with his face a blank, nodded and Roger Ellison departed.

As Peter closed the door behind him, I burst out, "But there *is* something you could have told him! You're afraid it was poison, aren't you?"

Peter finished his coffee and poured out another cup. "God knows. It seems to me, whatever the truth is, I did the wrong thing. If it was her heart, then the worst thing I could have done for her was dragging her over here when she was tired. And if by any chance it was poison, then I was too late. My miserable brain worked too slowly. She'd had her hot drink, as she told us, and there may have been something in it."

"Suppose there was something in that drink," I said, "then it could only have been Grace or Beryl who gave it to her, couldn't it? Didn't the others go back to The Green Man for dinner?"

"Oh no, they were all there," Peter said. "Grace was giving them dinner—Martin, Luke and Vanessa, as well as Beryl. I don't know who made the drink or who carried it up to Henrietta, or who had a chance of getting at it for a moment. I mean, suppose whoever was taking it up to her put it down somewhere and went back to the kitchen for something, one of the others could have dropped the poison into it. But I can tell you one thing, if it was Grace, Martin or Luke, you'll never get the truth out of them. They'll all cover up for each other."

"You don't think they'd cover up for Beryl?"

"I'm not sure."

"Or you, if they thought it was you?"

"Somehow I don't think so. I don't think they've ever quite forgiven Beryl and me for existing. But perhaps I'm wrong. Perhaps it's she and I who haven't forgiven them for being there already when we arrived."

"And perhaps none of you forgave Henrietta for coming on the scene."

His hand, holding the coffee cup, jerked slightly and slopped some coffee into the saucer. "Is that what you really think—of me, I mean?"

"Of course not. I was only taking your argument to its logical conclusion. Somehow I don't think anyone killed Henrietta because they objected to having a stepmother. If they killed her at all. Roger may be right; it was her heart."

"Brought on by the fire?"

"Yes . . ." Suddenly I seemed to hear myself and Peter talking of Henrietta's death when Henrietta herself, the best of friends, lost to us both for ever, lay upstairs, and it struck me that our voices sounded incredibly callous and indifferent. Yet this was not true of us. Shock had numbed us, but presently pain would come, and for the moment, possibly, it was just as well that we could maintain our apparent detachment. "We'd better telephone Grace."

"Yes."

"D'you want me to do it?"

"No, it's all right, I will." He put down his cup, picked up the telephone and dialled.

Someone answered almost at once, Grace, I assumed. He told her briefly what had happened and she seemed to have very little to say in reply, and when Peter asked her if she would inform the other Cosgroves, it appeared she agreed. That was all.

He put the telephone down and said, "She's coming round."

"What about the others?"

"Beryl's gone off to work, but Grace is going to phone her," he said, "and also The Green Man. I suppose they'll all come here too. And the undertaker. And then we'll have to arrange about the funeral. Oh God . . ." He suddenly caught hold of me and pulled me to him. "I loved that old woman, I really loved her. If any of them killed her, I don't care who it is, I'll—I'll—" But his voice choked and he could not bring himself to say what he would do. Letting me go, he turned away to the window and stood looking out of it, his back to the room.

He was still standing there when I heard the sound of a car in the lane.

"There's Grace already," I said.

"No," he answered, moving away from the window to the door, "it's Beddowes and Mason."

Opening the door, he waited on the threshold to greet the two detectives as they walked up the garden path.

As they came in at the door the swiftly moving little eyes of Superintendent Beddowes roved all round the room before they came to rest on my face, but it was only for an instant that they stayed there. His face was grave and so was the face of Sergeant Mason. They had just encountered Dr. Ellison in the lane, the superintendent explained, and he had stopped his car to tell them of the death of Mrs. Cosgrove. He offered sympathy, said that Mrs. Cosgrove

had been a wonderful old lady and that it was truly sad
that the events of the last few days had been too much for
her, but that that was hardly surprising. They might have
been too much for a far younger woman, anyway if she
had a bad heart, as he believed Mrs. Cosgrove had had.
Meanwhile his gaze had settled with a certain intentness on
the coffee-pot.

I asked him if he and the sergeant would like coffee and
when the offer was gratefully accepted, I said that I had
better warm it up and took the pot out to the kitchen.
While I was there I heard the tramp of the two men on the
staircase and realized that they were going up to take a
look at Henrietta, but they stayed upstairs only for a minute or two and when I returned to the living-room with the
coffee and two more cups, the superintendent was saying to
Peter that it seemed at least that Mrs. Cosgrove had died
peacefully in her sleep, and that that was something to be
thankful for.

"But I'd gathered somehow she was staying with Mrs.
Kenworthy in the village," he said. "She changed her mind,
did she?"

"Yes," Peter said.

"Any reason for it, that you know of?" Mr. Beddowes
asked.

"She may have felt she'd find things quieter here," Peter
said. "My brothers and my sister-in-law were actually staying at The Green Man, but I think they were spending
most of their time with my sister."

"Yes, I see," Mr. Beddowes said. "Very interesting to
meet your brother, Mr. Martin Cosgrove. I've seen him on
television in one of those Shakespeare things—*Macbeth*, I
think it was. Yes, that's right, it was *Macbeth*. Queer feeling, meeting him, because I couldn't help feeling he'd start
spouting in blank verse any minute and that for all I knew,
he'd a habit of committing murder. Twenty mortal
murders, isn't that what it says? He's so like he is on the

screen. But naturally I'd murder on my mind, and that's
what I came here to see you and Mrs. Cosgrove about—I
mean young Mrs. Cosgrove—because I've some information from London about your friend, Mr. Edge, and I'd be
glad if there's anything you can add to it."

We had all sat down and the superintendent and the sergeant were sipping their coffee.

"I'll do my best," Peter said.

"There are two things," Mr. Beddowes went on. "First, it
seems there were a good many pictures in his studio and
our man who went there says he had a queer feeling about
them right away, he didn't quite know why, but it happens
he knows quite a lot about such things, and he decided it
would be best to get an expert to look at them. So he got in
a man who's done a certain amount of that sort of work for
the police before, and he said without hesitation they were
forgeries of an artist called Francis Buller. Quite clever forgeries, he said, but he hadn't a doubt in his mind that was
all they were. If they'd been genuine, it seems, they'd have
been worth quite a bit of money, but as it was they were
worthless. Now would you have any idea about that?"

Peter took some time to reply. I was thankful that it was
at him that both the detectives were looking and not at me.
I was ready to support Peter in whatever he decided to say,
but I would not have liked just then to have to think of an
answer myself.

"You think this has something to do with his murder?"
Peter said.

"Not necessarily," Mr. Beddowes answered. "I'm just
trying to sort out what kind of man he was and the kind of
contacts he may have had, because that's an important
matter when it comes to an investigation of this sort."

"Yes, of course. Well, if you want to know if I'd any
knowledge of these forgeries," Peter said, "yes, I'd a pretty
strong suspicion he was turning them out. I don't know if
anyone's mentioned it to you, but my stepmother had two

Francis Bullers, and I'd always had my doubts of them. And if you ask Mr. Ormerod about them, he'll tell you he was put on the trail of them by Simon Edge. It was Ormerod who sold them to my stepmother. And it happens I'd told Edge an American collector called Everett Baynes was coming to take a look at them and would probably buy them if they were genuine, and it's struck me since that, that may have scared Edge and that he had an idea he might be able to steal them back before Baynes arrived, and that that's why he was outside my stepmother's house when the fire started."

"And saw who started it and thought he could levy blackmail, and got murdered for his pains," Mr. Beddowes said.

"That's what seems probable to me," Peter said.

"That's very interesting." The superintendent darted one of his swift glances at the sergeant, as if to see if he also thought it interesting, and what he saw seemed to satisfy him, for he went on, "As a matter of fact, I was just coming to the subject of blackmail. A number of letters, photographs and so on, were found in Mr. Edge's studio which suggest he may have gone in for it now and then. Had you any suspicion of that, Mr. Cosgrove?" His tone had suddenly hardened and the appearance of sympathetic friendliness had gone from his eyes.

Peter seemed singularly unperturbed. "Are you asking me if I was an accessory to the crime?" he inquired.

The superintendent placed a large hand on each of his knees and leant forward. "To me, blackmail's a much more serious crime than forging a few paintings that take in simple-minded people who don't know better."

"I agree with you," Peter said.

"But you claim you'd no suspicion it was one of your friend's sidelines?"

"None whatever, till his murder, when it seemed to give someone a possible motive."

"If you'd found it out, what would you have done?"

"I doubt if that's a fair question," Peter said, "but I think I'd have arranged that he ceased to be one of my friends."

"Although you tolerated his selling forgeries to your stepmother."

"I thought we'd agreed that wasn't as serious as blackmail."

"But Mrs. Cosgrove wasn't a rich woman, was she? Didn't you mind her throwing her money away on worthless fakes?"

I could see the little sparks in Peter's eyes that meant that his temper was rising.

"To begin with," he said, "at the time she bought them I didn't know they were fakes. I'm no expert myself, and I only began to suspect what they were because of an odd thing about a yew tree in one of them. And I didn't know Ormerod had got them from Edge. Apart from that—"

"Ah, apart from that," Mr. Beddowes interrupted and his tone was bland again, "Mr. Edge was a very old friend of yours and it was your instinct to be loyal to him. Loyalty's an admirable thing, Mr. Cosgrove. Don't imagine I don't think so. But sometimes a murderer's wife or mother is so loyal to him that other women die. And sometimes a man goes to prison and keeps silence for years sooner than betray the others who were in on his crime with him, and so they can go on robbing banks, or setting off bombs, killing innocent people, whatever their specialty happens to be. And so on, if you take my meaning."

Peter was controlling himself with difficulty. "I believe your meaning is that you think I'm covering up for Simon's murderer."

"No, no, I don't see why you should think that," Mr. Beddowes said. He stood up and the sergeant immediately stood up too. "I'm sure you don't know any more about it than I do. Perhaps less. I've the names of a few people who appear to have been paying him blackmail and one of them actually happens to be a Pakistani woman with a strong foreign accent who we've found is in this country with forged papers. She might have made that telephone call you told me about, which sent us chasing after that unfortunate German woman. So you see, our murderer may not have been based in these parts at all. He or she may have traced him down here from London. All the same . . ." He paused to make what he said sound weightier. "I've a feeling you may know a little more, or have doubts about a few more things than you've admitted. I can't tell you why I have the feeling. It's just what's commonly called a hunch, though perhaps a writing man like yourself would prefer a word like intuition. But if I happen to be right, please do some careful thinking."

He turned to me with a little bow, as if he were apologizing for having left me out of the conversation, then opened the door and he and the sergeant stepped out into the garden. Peter shut the door after them with what was almost a slam.

"So he's made up his mind it's one of us!" he exploded.

My first instinct was to say, "Sh!" because it seemed wrong to speak in even a normal tone of voice with Henrietta in the room upstairs, and almost to shout, as Peter just had, seemed shocking beyond words. I added, "And unfortunately you agree with him."

"But I didn't know of the London angle," Peter said. "If Simon was really playing around with blackmail, his murderer could have come from anywhere."

"And the fire was just a coincidence, perhaps not even arson, perhaps really just a fault in the wiring."

"Why not?"

"And Henrietta's death was just her heart giving out?"

"That's what Roger thinks."

"But you don't, Peter. You know you don't."

He dropped into a chair. "All right, I don't. And if there weren't one or two things I don't understand, I'd be ready to swear I know who's at the bottom of everything."

"You might have said that to Beddowes."

He shook his head. "Not till I'm certain. And even then, if it were only Simon, if it weren't for Henrietta . . ." He gave another little shake of his head, which this time seemed to be in answer to something that had passed through his own mind and puzzled him.

Once more there were the sounds of footsteps on the path outside. This time I looked out of the window and said, "It's Grace."

Grace came in with an oddly apprehensive air. At first she said nothing, but only crossed to the fire and standing in front of it, gave a sharp shiver, as if the short walk from the village had chilled her to the bone, although the morning was not really cold. After a moment she said questioningly, "Well?"

Neither Peter nor I seemed able to think of an answer to that, so we said nothing.

Grace gave a sigh that sounded very sad. "She's upstairs, is she?" she said.

"Yes," I said. "D'you want to go up to her?"

"Yes—oh yes, if she's still here," Grace answered.

"Why shouldn't she be?" Peter asked.

"I just wondered . . . the police . . . I wondered if . . ." She did not seem able to finish.

"You wondered if they'd taken her away to the mortuary for a post mortem," Peter said.

"But they haven't?"

"Why should they? Roger's going to sign the death certificate."

"Saying it was her heart?"

"Yes."

"And he's sure?"

He gave her a thoughtful look. "Why aren't you, Grace?"

"Oh, I don't know anything about it," she said quickly. "How could I? I suppose it's just a state of mind I've got into—the fire, the murder, your fire here, that poor Klein woman going around the bend. It makes one expect things to be—well, all wrong somehow. Everything. Stupid of one, of course, and of course I could see yesterday that things had got to be too much for Henrietta, and in a way it wasn't a surprise to hear she'd died, but all the same . . ." Grace moved away from the fire towards the staircase. "I'll go up now, shall I?"

She still had her unfamiliar air almost of fearfulness. Usually she looked so strong, so sure of herself, that it made me wonder if she was one of the people who are really deeply afraid of the dead.

"Shall I come with you?" I suggested.

"No," Grace said. "I'll just—well, I suppose I just want to see her and say goodbye. Just a minute."

She went to the stairs. But I could hear that half way up them she stood still, as if she had to nerve herself to go on. Then suddenly she went on rapidly, yet after that there was no sound of footsteps overhead. She must have stood still in the doorway, looking across the room at Henrietta without moving for at least five minutes. When she came down again she moved slowly, exhausted, it seemed, by what she had just experienced. There were tears in her eyes which she dabbed at with a handkerchief.

She spoke to Peter. "Did you ever think of her as a mother, Peter, or only as a friend?"

"A friend," he said. "I was too old already when father married her to accept her as a mother. Besides, I remembered my own mother too well. But I was very fond of her."

"So was I," Grace said. "She was one of my best friends.

I'll miss her dreadfully." She sat down. "We'll have to arrange the funeral, shan't we? I wonder which she wanted, to be buried or cremated. Somehow I think she'd have preferred cremation."

"For that I believe you have to get two doctors to sign the death certificate," Peter said.

"Yes—yes, I believe you do." There was a trace of dismay in Grace's voice. "But there's no doubt, is there? I mean, it was her heart."

"All I can say is, that's what Roger thinks," he answered. "Or says he thinks."

"You mean he *isn't* sure?" she said swiftly.

He shook his head. "I'm just getting like you, Grace, feeling almost anything may be wrong because there've been so many events recently that definitely are."

She leant her head back and closed her eyes and seemed to be trying to relax, though her heavy eyebrows were drawn together, giving her face a look of tension. There were still the marks of tears on her cheeks. Without opening her eyes, she said, "I suppose you know Beryl and Max are getting married."

"Yes," he answered.

"What d'you think about it?"

"I'm sorry she doesn't seem more enthusiastic about it than she does."

"Did she tell you she's pregnant?"

"Yes."

"She doesn't seem very enthusiastic about that either, does she?"

"In the circumstances I don't suppose you can expect her to be. I don't think she'd marry if it hadn't happened."

"It's always seemed to me she and Max were perfectly suited to each other," Grace said. "I've wished for ages they'd wake up to the fact themselves, and I think Henrietta did too, but we gave up hope long ago. It's amusing, isn't it, that they've been lovers so long without any of us suspecting it?"

"Amusing?"

"Well, it's made fools of us all in a way, hasn't it? I mean, we've been so wrong about them."

"I don't think I've ever understood either of them," Peter said. "Beryl and I never had much interest in each other when we were children, and I've always thought of Max as a nervy sort of character who was scared of his own shadow. But look at how he went up that ladder into the fire."

I offered my own theory. "Isn't it just that very introverted sort of person who sometimes does the most heroic things?"

Grace opened her eyes and sat upright. "That's the Bentley arriving," she said. "The others have got here at last."

*

Vanessa led the way in, followed by Luke and after a moment by Martin, who seemed to prefer to make an entrance by himself. Vanessa looked the most agitated of the three, Luke the most distressed and Martin the grimmest. He took up a stand in the middle of the room and when Peter asked if any of them wanted to go upstairs to see Henrietta for a last time, he merely stared before him as if he had not heard. It was only Vanessa who decided to go up, but she could hardly have glanced into the room, for she came downstairs again almost immediately.

"So that's that," Martin observed, as if Vanessa had acted for the three of them. "Aren't you going to give us a drink, Peter?"

Peter replied by asking them what they wanted and all of them chose whisky. When he looked at me questioningly, I shook my head. I found that for some reason the thought of a drink repelled me. I had a feeling that in another moment they would all be drinking a toast to Henrietta's memory and that this would be unbearable. However, I was quite wrong about them, for Vanessa no sooner had her drink in her hand than she rattled her bracelets and said, "What I want to know is, what did you and Freda give Henrietta last night, Peter?"

He looked at her uncomprehendingly, while I said, "Why don't you all sit down?"

Martin flung himself down on the sofa, managing with a touch of majesty to look detached from the rest of them, absorbed in thoughts of his own. Luke sat down in a chair and Vanessa remained standing and repeated her question, "Well, what did you give her?"

"I gave her whisky," Peter said. "Why? It was what she asked for."

"And what was in the whisky?" she asked.

"What was in . . . ?" He began to understand her. "Oh, my God, what idea have you got into your head now?"

"A very natural idea," she replied. Her pale, oval face was set. "I don't have to explain, do I?"

"I'd just as soon you didn't, if you mean what I think you mean," he said.

"Of course I mean it," she said. "I want to know what you put into the whisky you gave Henrietta last night."

"A small amount of water," he said. "That was how she liked it."

"Please be serious," she said sharply. "You can see it's unavoidable for us to suspect you. You came to Grace's house mysteriously yesterday evening, removed Henrietta, didn't let Beryl see her when she came here, and then she died in her sleep. So I want to know quite simply, are you going to tell us what you used, or have we got to leave it to the police to find out?"

Martin came abruptly out of his abstraction. "What the hell is the woman talking about? Luke, can't you make her keep quiet?" He seemed always to prefer to talk to Vanessa in the third person, through Luke or somebody else.

"It's all right, she's just a bit wound up," Luke said. "She'll run down presently."

"I don't understand her," Martin said. "I never do. She always talks the most God-awful nonsense."

"She's only decided Freda and I poisoned Henrietta," Peter said. "It's quite simple."

"And did you?" Martin asked.

"As a matter of fact, no," Peter said.

"You can talk quite freely here, you know," Martin told him. "It's all in the family."

"The family, the family!" Vanessa shrieked, her bracelets jangling. "The Cosgroves think you can cover up anything for each other. Skeletons in cupboards and I don't know what else. But I am not a Cosgrove and I have some belief in truth and justice. I believe Henrietta was poisoned and I think there should be a post mortem."

Grace put a hand up quickly to her mouth. "Oh no, not a post mortem—oh no! Cutting the poor woman up, doing awful things to her. They send your organs off to a laboratory and stitch you up with awful great tacking stitches—oh no!"

Vanessa turned to her sternly. "But if this was murder, don't you want it discovered?"

"If it was," Peter said, "I'm with you, Vanessa. I do want it discovered. But I'm not the murderer. After all, as I think you'll agree, I haven't any motive for wanting Henrietta dead."

"But it was your motive that made me think of it," she said. "It's so obvious."

"I'm sorry," he said, "I don't follow you."

"But we saw you, we *saw* you, Luke and I," she said.

Peter gave his head a bewildered shake. "Saw me when and where?"

"We saw you making off with the pictures," she said.

"The Bullers. We saw you come sneaking out of the house, carrying something bulky under your arm. And that's what it was, wasn't it, the two Bullers? And Henrietta saw you and she was going to make you give them back to her. But they're worth quite a lot of money and if ever I saw two people who need money, it's you and Freda. So you decided to keep them. And to silence Henrietta, you got her here last night and gave her something in her whisky, an overdose of sleeping pills or something, or perhaps you put a plastic bag over her head and smothered her, or held a pillow over her face when she was too weak to fight back, or something like that—anything that would make that man Ellison say it was her heart giving out after the strain of the last few days. Don't try to argue your way out of it. I tell you, Luke and I saw you."

"Wait a minute!" My brain stimulated by the attack on Peter, I came abruptly into the discussion. "Suppose you saw him come out of the house, what were you and Luke doing there? We were given to understand you spent the evening playing bridge with Grace and Martin."

"That was later on," Vanessa said. "But first we went for a short walk. We thought we'd like some fresh air and we went for a stroll, and we came down this lane and we saw what I've just told you—Peter coming out of the house carrying a square sort of parcel which I'm sure was the two Bullers."

"That puts you on the spot dangerously close to the time the fire started," I said.

"By God, it does!" Martin exclaimed. "Luke, I told you, you should keep the woman quiet."

"But I'm afraid she's right, you know," Luke said in his mild way. "We did see you, Peter."

Peter threw his hands out in a gesture of defeat. "All right, you did. I admit it. I took the Bullers. Only they weren't Bullers and that's the reason I took them."

Martin tossed off his whisky and held out his glass for a refill.

"I'm afraid you'll have to be more explicit than that," he said. Seated on the sofa, almost as if on a dais above the rest of us, he had managed to assume a magisterial air, dominating the situation. "It's not very illuminating."

Peter poured out another drink for him.

"I'll explain," he said. "Henrietta's Bullers were fakes. They were painted by Simon Edge. He managed to palm them off on Max, who sold them, I think in good faith, to Henrietta. But I always had my suspicions of them. I knew Simon wasn't above a bit of forgery and that Buller was one of his lines. And I was never happy about the yew tree in front of the church. That was one of Simon's blunders. He painted it just as it is now, not as it might have been a hundred years ago. So when Henrietta told us all an expert was coming to look at the pictures, I thought that was certain to lead to trouble for Simon, who, after all, was a very old friend of mine. So on an impulse I removed them. A damn silly impulse, but there it is, I did it. I meant to have them turn up somewhere once the expert was safely out of the country and be returned to Henrietta. And I'm quite certain she didn't see me take them. If she had, she'd have said something to me about it, which she never did. And the one thing you can be sure of, Vanessa's wrong, I couldn't possibly have made any money out of them."

"In that case," Vanessa said, "where are they now? How are we to be sure they're fakes? I think we should have them examined to see if any of this is true, or if in fact they're worth a great deal."

"I'm afraid you're too late for that," Peter said. "You can have the remnants of them, if you like, which are in our dustbin. The rest of them went up in smoke when Ilse Klein tried to set fire to our garage."

"Convenient for you—" Vanessa began, but was interrupted by the ringing of the doorbell.

We had all been so intent on one another that we had not heard the footsteps approaching the door outside. When Peter opened it Beryl and Max came in. I thought there was a look of closeness about them that I had never noticed before, yet I wondered at myself now for not having done so. It had been there for a long time, I realized, but I had never troubled to think about it.

"We came as soon as we got your message, Grace," Max said. His face gave one of its more violent twitches. "It's really true, is it? Henrietta's dead?"

"Oh yes, it's true," Peter answered.

"It's difficult to take in, somehow," Max said. "There was such life in her. It was her heart, was it?"

"So Roger Ellison says," Peter said.

"I was afraid of something of the sort last night." Beryl looked listless and sad. "That's to say, I didn't exactly expect it, but I was worried."

"But it isn't true it was heart, I'm certain it isn't!" Vanessa broke in fiercely. "I'm going to the police. I don't know what the procedure is, but I'm going to insist on a post mortem, because I'm certain Henrietta was poisoned. I'm sure I'm right. Peter stole the Bullers, went back and set fire to the house to conceal the theft, Henrietta saw him and so he abducted her from Grace's house last night and gave her whisky laced with something that killed her. And if any of you says again, let's keep it in the family, I shall start to scream—I shall scream and scream!"

"She won't really, you know," Luke said. "It's just an expression she uses. She can always keep her head in a crisis. I've never heard her scream in my life."

"Well, this is once you're going to," she said. "I want the truth. Martin, will you please drive me into Alcaster now? I don't think we should waste any more time. I want to talk to that man Beddowes."

Again the attack on Peter sharpened my wits. Something that Simon had said on the morning after the fire came back to me. Something about the motive for the lighting of the fire having possibly been revenge.

"Don't be in such a hurry," I said. "There's something we might clear up first. I think by your own admission, Vanessa, you and Luke were near the house when Peter made off with the pictures."

"Haven't I said we were?" she said.

"Then, as I said a moment ago," I went on rapidly, "you were on the spot dangerously close to the time the fire started, and I don't see why it shouldn't have been you who started it. If you piled up some sort of slow-burning stuff over the can of petrol, as Ilse did in our garage, you could have got back to your game of bridge before the fire really took hold on the house and got noticed by anyone. And you had a motive. You've always detested Martin, haven't you? He never misses a chance of jeering at you and making you look a fool. If I were you, I think I'd hate him. And all that may have angered Luke as much as it did you, besides which it's possible, isn't it, that he's always been jealous of Martin? Luke started in the theatre but couldn't make it, and he got out and he's depended on you ever since. If you wanted revenge on Martin for all his mockery, if you wanted the death of Louise exposed, I'm not sure he'd stop you." I became more and more sure of myself as I went on, though hating myself for it, because Luke had always been my favourite of the three elder Cosgroves. "I know you've claimed you knew nothing about the skeleton in the cupboard," I continued, "but I think Luke may have told you all about it. I'm not saying you intended to kill Henrietta. It probably didn't occur to you that she'd be upstairs and get trapped. But if it hadn't been for the miracle of Max getting to the house in time, you would have killed her, and indirectly perhaps you did, because if she hadn't had to go through what she did this last day or two, she'd probably still be alive and well. Let's forget about poison. It was death from over-strain. I don't know if you can call that murder, but in its way it's what you achieved, so don't try to blame Peter for it."

"Wait, wait!" It was Grace who broke in this time, her deep voice cracking into unfamiliar shrillness. "Before you go on hurling accusations at one another, there's something you ought to know. I've been sitting here wondering if I'd got to talk about it, though I knew of course I'd have to sooner or later, but it felt so awful, knowing I must, I've been trying to put it off. It was wrong of me. I ought to have told you all about it as soon as I got here. You're wrong, Freda, Henrietta didn't die of over-strain. She *was* poisoned. But you're wrong too, Vanessa, she didn't get the poison in this house. It happened in mine. You see, my morphia's missing."

Martin jerked upright on the sofa, on which he had dropped into a half-reclining position.

"Your *what*, Grace?"

"My morphia," she said.

"But what in the world did you have morphia around the place for?" he asked. "It isn't a thing one normally keeps, as one does aspirins or indigestion tablets."

"Well, it's a little difficult to explain," she said, "but the fact is, I've had it for a long time. Ever since Edmund was killed, actually. You see, when Roger took over Edmund's practice, I handed all Edmund's drugs over to him except the morphia. Something made me keep it. I was so full of despair at the time, I felt so lost without Edmund, I thought seriously of taking my own life. Truly I did. And then I began to get over things bit by bit and sometimes I'd look at the bottle of morphia in my bathroom cabinet and say to myself I really ought to get rid of it. But something always stopped me throwing it away. I'd think, suppose I had some awful illness that I knew wasn't curable, something that might paralyze me, for instance, and make me helpless, or suppose I went blind or found my mind was going, mightn't it be nice just to be able to finish things off quickly? So I'd leave the bottle where it was. And there it's been all this time, until today. I mean, it was today I missed it. I suppose it was taken last night and some of it got into the hot drink I made for Henrietta."

"You really do astonish me, Grace," Martin said. There was a sympathy in his voice which was evoked in him by few people but his elder sister. "I'd never have dreamt you'd ever contemplated suicide. You always seemed able to cope with everything so wonderfully. If I'd realized, my dear, if I could have done anything at all to help . . . But the question is now, how many people knew you had a supply of morphia? How many did you tell about it?"

"No one at all," she said uneasily. "But the fact is . . ."

"Yes?" he said.

"Well, you were all in and out of my bathroom yesterday," she said. "If someone had thought of poisoning Henrietta, they might have looked in the cabinet to see if I'd any sleeping pills they could use. And there the morphia was, labelled of course."

"Well, I didn't look in your bathroom cabinet," Vanessa said. "I knew nothing about any morphia until this moment. And not a word that Freda said is true. I didn't know the skeleton existed till the police told us about it, and I don't hate Martin, I really admire him very much. I know he doesn't mean half the things he says to me."

"That's true, you know," Martin said. "Vanessa and I understand one another. The things we say are just a kind of game we play."

I heard Peter draw a shuddering breath, as if he were trying to nerve himself to speak. He put an arm round my shoulders. "It was a good try, Freda, but they're right, you know. Vanessa had nothing to do with the fire or either murder. And there's something else you were wrong about, something we might have thought of sooner. It wasn't a miracle that Max arrived on the scene in time to save Henrietta. The miracle was that Simon did."

Beryl opened her mouth as if she were about to say something, but then she closed it again. She gave Max a long, hard stare.

"Oh yes," Peter went on. "Simon had gone to the house to get back his paintings before Everett Baynes arrived, and he saw Max light the fire. I don't think Simon understood his motive. He probably thought it was something to do with the pictures. But I think he must also have seen Beryl come out of the house and talk to Max and then go in again, so that she could come tumbling out later as if she'd almost been trapped. He must have known she was in on it, because he wasn't surprised when she telephoned him with her voice disguised to arrange that meeting at the dig. But crook though Simon was, he wouldn't stand for murder, which was what the fire was meant to be all along. So he told Max if he didn't get the ladder and save Henrietta, he'd do it himself. Isn't that how it happened, Max? Didn't you realize that if she wasn't going to die in the fire, it would pay you best to be the one who saved her? Then, if you made another attempt to kill her later, you wouldn't be suspected. I think I've known this ever since Simon was killed, though I didn't understand the motive till Beryl told us she was pregnant and would have to give up her job. You needed the insurance money on the house that Henrietta had left to Beryl, but you couldn't get it soon unless Henrietta died. And I acted too slowly when I guessed she was in danger. The drug was beginning to affect her by the time she got here. Freda had to help her upstairs. Henrietta thought it was the whisky, but of course it was the morphia. She was a dead woman already by the time I brought her here. And I may have been so slow because Beryl's my sister and I was doing my best not to believe any of this. But though she's my sister, not even a stepsister, this is something that isn't going to be kept in the family."

CHAPTER 10

Beryl took a quick step away from Max, as if his nearness had become intolerable to her. Her round, plump face was sullen.

"Didn't I tell you it wouldn't work?" she said. "I should never have listened to you. We could have managed without the money."

"Be quiet!" he said sharply. "This is all moonshine. There's no proof of any of it."

"There will be when they open the old woman up and find the morphia inside her," she said.

"But why need they do that? I think we can do a deal." Max turned to Martin. "Can't we?"

Martin gave him a look of cold surprise. "Are you addressing me?"

"Of course," Max said.

"I can't imagine why. What deal can you possibly offer?"

"It's quite simple," Max said. "You forget this ingenious theory of Peter's and I forget the existence of the cupboard with the skeleton in it."

"I see." Martin frowned heavily. "You tell the police there was no cupboard in the passage upstairs all the time you and your parents lived in the house, so the skeleton of poor Louise can't possibly be connected with me, and we allow you to get away with two murders."

"And Beryl and I go away," Max said. "You needn't always be coming face to face with us and having your consciences troubled. We were thinking of going away anyway. It was partly why we needed money. I've known for some time the villa was doomed. Did I tell you about that? It was settled at a meeting I was at on Thursday. The bulldozers are going in and the site's going to be flattened and council houses built on it. It's a little more than I can bear. It's true we've got almost everything of interest out of the place, but it's still got a meaning for me that I don't suppose you can understand, and with it gone I've no wish to stay on in Alcaster. I've already written my letter of resignation. But I've no other job lined up yet and we'll need money to tide us over till I get something. So you can see the deal I suggested would be to the advantage of all of us."

"I see," Martin said again. "Thank you, Max. Thank you for making my mind up for me." He rose to his feet. In the strange way that he had, he managed to look several inches taller than he was, an upright, powerful figure. He went on, "Your suggestion, of course, is monstrous. That's so clear that I see plainly at last the only path open to me. I've been hesitating, hoping I might be able to think of some way out of my difficulty, but the truth is, there is none. So I shall go to the police and tell them the truth. Grace and Luke will no doubt go with me and confirm the fact that Louise was not murdered, but I don't know what the outcome will be. A very serious matter for me, I have no doubt, but there's some relief in having made up my mind at last. This thing has hung over me for twenty years, and I've always felt that sooner or later it was bound to be exposed. And we will all demand a post mortem on Henrietta."

"But it's so unnecessary." Max's tone was quiet and reasonable. "She died quietly and peacefully. Probably being killed by another heart attack, which was bound to happen soon, would have been far more frightening and painful. Ellison will sign a death certificate, so there won't be any inquest. And Simon Edge was a nasty little crook. Do any of you really care about his death? I'm sure I'm not the only person he tried to blackmail, and if the police find out it was one of his lines, as perhaps they have already, they'll probably end up deciding his murderer was one of his other victims, even if they never manage to trace him. The whole affair can be forgotten, while I forget the cupboard. So the British stage can keep one of its brightest ornaments and Beryl and I can go far away, abroad perhaps, and if you'd sooner not know where we are, we won't even send you the occasional Christmas card."

"I'm not going anywhere with you," Beryl said in a low, husky voice. There were patches of red on her cheeks and her eyes had an unnatural stare in them. "Can't you see you haven't a chance of persuading them to let you get away with it? You're such a fool. You've never been able to think of anything but your damned villa. You've never understood what was going on round you in the real world. No, I'm not going with you, I'm going by myself, and luckily I've some morphia left and I can think of a good use for it."

She went quickly to the door and pulled it open.

Peter took a step after her. "Beryl—"

Martin caught him by the arm and held him back.

"Let her go," he said quietly.

Peter stood still and she walked off down the garden path. As we listened in silence we heard a car start up.

Sounding both surprised and helpless, Max observed, "She's taken the car."

"I'll drive you to the police station in Alcaster, if you like," Martin said. "That's where I'm going myself."

"Thank you, I think I'll just walk up to the dig." A curious vagueness had come into Max's manner. It did not seem to occur to him that anyone might stop him. "You can tell them they'll find me there."

"Alive or dead?" Martin asked brutally.

"I must think it over," Max said. "If I'm dead, of course, I shan't be able to tell them about the cupboard, and I feel, all things considered, that they really ought to know about it."

"Don't let that thought affect your decision," Martin said. "I've said I'm going to them and you can rely on me to do so."

"Oh, it's nothing to me in itself," Max said. "Anyway, I can always put it in writing. So do what you like."

He turned to the door. As he wandered out he still had the air of vagueness, of not knowing and not much caring where he was going, that had come to him a moment before. We heard the garden gate squeak as he opened it and then clang shut behind him.

Martin let go of Peter's arm, which he had kept hold of, at first to restrain him, but then as if he himself felt a need for the support it gave him.

"Well, here we go," he said. "Grace, Luke, are you coming with me?"

Grace looked up at him with a haggard face and tears in her eyes. "Of course."

"Yes, naturally," Luke said.

"I'll come too," Vanessa said. "I wasn't a witness when Louise fell downstairs, but I may be useful."

"Thank you, Vanessa," Martin said. "I'm sure you will be."

I suddenly felt moved to break in. "But Martin, why don't you wait a little while to see what Max does? He may not put it in writing after all. And what good will it do anyone to have everything dragged into the open now?"

He laid a hand on my shoulder. "It'll do me a certain amount of good. Anyway, it's what I'm going to do. I knew that the moment he offered me that shabby deal. So goodbye, anyway for the present. I'm not sure when we'll be able to meet again. That's a pity, when we were just beginning to get to know one another. Even Peter and I seem to be better friends than we were. Perhaps you'll both call on me occasionally in my new abode, wherever that turns out to be."

He smiled, and the smile was only very slightly dramatic, as he turned to the door. Grace, crying without restraint, and Luke and Vanessa followed him out.

It was only about an hour later that the van from the mortuary and some quiet, competent men arrived to collect Henrietta's body. Most of that time Peter and I had sat side by side on the sofa, holding each other, but hardly talking, feeling, now that we were alone in the cottage with her, that Henrietta's silence imposed silence on us.

At one point I had said, "What will they do to him?"

"I don't know," Peter had answered. "I believe sometimes if an offence happened very long ago, with witnesses who've died or can't be traced, it's decided it's not in the public interest to bring a charge. I think I read that somewhere. But how it works when you've got someone determined to make a confession, I don't know. Even at the worst, I shouldn't think it'll mean a heavy sentence, but I suppose it'll smash his career. Anyway, for a while. We live in broadminded times, or do I simply mean we've all become rather good at forgetting? In the end I think his public will welcome him back. What's more on my mind is what Beryl's going to do. That morphia she said she kept . . ."

"She kept it on purpose, of course," I had said, "to make sure she had a way out if she found she couldn't live with what she'd done."

"Yes," Peter had agreed, and we had fallen silent again.

It was not until after the van had come and gone and we had had our usual lunch of sandwiches, made coffee and returned with it to the living-room that we said any more to one another than the few odd words about the things that we happened to be doing, none of them touching on the events of the day.

But at last I said, "D'you think Luke will ever forgive me for trying to prove he and Vanessa were the murderers?"

"Oh, I should think so," Peter said, "if I forgive Vanessa."

"You know, I never would have believed Max had it in him to commit a murder if I hadn't seen him climbing the ladder to rescue Henrietta," I went on. "I mean, he seemed so negative. But it seems to me that people who are capable of acts of extraordinary bravery may also be bold enough to commit acts of extraordinary evil. The only things they're really and truly scared of are the things that seem to most of us normally human."

Peter was putting sugar into his coffee. "He really had amazing bad luck, hadn't he?" he said. "First and of course the worst thing was Simon being on the scene. But then there was also the fact that on just the night when he'd decided to burn the house down, Ilse went to the doctor. He meant her to be blamed for the fire, of course, from the time he caught her trying to set fire to his office out at the dig. In fact, I imagine it was catching her there that put the idea of a fire into his head as a way of getting rid of Henrietta. He was sure Ilse would be blamed, once the police found out she was our local fire-bug, because in the normal course of events she wouldn't have had an alibi. He knew her well enough to know that she almost never went out in the evening. That she'd go to the doctor on just that Wednesday was something he couldn't anticipate. Then Louise's skeleton was really another bit of misfortune. I think he chose the evening of Henrietta's birthday party for his job because all the family was going to be here, and he thought that that would provide a nice collection of suspects if his scheme about Ilse went wrong. But, in fact, they were the last people who'd have wanted to burn the house down, just because they'd have known the skeleton might be discovered. Yes, he had bad luck."

"You sound almost sorry for him," I said.

"Oh no, not that," Peter said, "if only because of what he made of Beryl."

"You don't think it was the other way round; that it was what she made of him?"

He considered it. "It could be. We'll never know. Perhaps she wanted to try murder, as she seems to have wanted to try sex and pregnancy and marriage—just to find out what she was missing. It's a thing most of us don't know."

"Or want to know."

"Well, perhaps I ought to know more about it than I do," he said. "I write about it, after all. I've three corpses in this thing I'm working on now, and I've been wondering recently if it wouldn't be a good idea to squeeze in another. I know the blood in them isn't the sticky stuff that comes out of human veins, it's just coloured red and comes out of an ink-bottle. All the same . . ."

"Yes?" I said, when he did not go on.

"I suppose you couldn't finish this book for me, could you?"

I gave a startled laugh. "Whatever put that idea into your head? You know I couldn't. I'm a cook, not a writer."

"The trouble is, I'm not sure if I'm going to be able to do it either," he said.

"Because of what's been happening to us?"

"Yes. I've been wondering . . ." He paused again. "D'you ever have the feeling I ought to try to get back into journalism, Freda?"

"I've never really thought about it," I said.

"If I did, we'd probably have more money than I'm making now."

"Is it what you want to do?"

"If you'd asked me a few days ago, I'd have said definitely no. Now I'm not so sure. But my books are never going to set the Thames on fire."

"You never know. And I don't think you could choose a worse time than now for making an important decision about a thing like that."

"I suppose not. But what about you?"

"What d'you mean, what about me?"

"How are you going to feel about staying on in Ickfield with all the talk and the pointing fingers there are going to be? Won't it be pretty painful? You might find London a splendidly anonymous place."

"Yes, of course staying here will be painful. But perhaps one ought to try to weather it. Or are you telling me you're feeling the pull of London yourself? I've always thought it would happen to you sooner or later."

He shook his head. "It isn't that. I've been very contented here. Incredibly contented. But that hasn't just been Ickfield, it's been you, and if it's been ruined for you, we aren't compelled to stay. I know you're right that this isn't a good time for making serious decisions, and before we did anything active about moving I'd like to get *The Screaming Spires* finished and off my mind—"

I interrupted, "I thought you were afraid you might not be able to finish it."

He gave a slightly sheepish smile. "Well, I am, but I expect I'll be able to get back to it after a while."

"Of course you will. You'll probably be at it tomorrow. You couldn't stop if you tried."

"You may be right. And after all, there's the money to be considered."

"Yes, it's always an excellent thing to do, to consider money."

"You're laughing at me."

I wanted to put my arms round him, but there was the coffee-table between us. I gave a sad shake of my head. "I don't feel very much like laughing at anything. But I think I'd put that fourth corpse in if I were you. An extra corpse is always refreshing."

M35

"On the other hand, one can overdo it. Perhaps three is enough." He put down his coffee cup and sat back, yawning. "What's for supper?"

"I don't know. I'll have to get something out of the freezer."

I would also have to do some hard thinking and some very hard work tomorrow, I realized. I was supposed to be producing the food for a dinner party on the day after, which some wealthy and very hospitable people in the village were giving for some of their friends. They were valuable clients and it would be foolish of me to let them down. They wanted smoked salmon, blanquette de veau and profiteroles with hot chocolate sauce. And I hadn't even done the shopping yet.

"We've some fillets of haddock, I think, and some chips," I said.

"Good," Peter said. "I like that."

ABOUT THE AUTHOR

E. X. FERRARS lives in Oxfordshire. She is the author of over forty works of mystery and suspense, including *Thinner Than Water, Experiment with Death,* and *Frog in the Throat.* She was recently given a special award by the British Crime Writers Association for continuing excellence in the mystery field.